ARABIAN
FURY

A PAT WALSH THRILLER

JAMES LAWRENCE

Arabian Fury is a work of fiction. Apart from the events and locales that figure in the narrative, all names, characters, places, and incidents are the products of the author's imagination or are used fictitiously. Any resemblance to current events, locales, or living persons is entirely coincidental.

ISBN-13: 978-1985699137
ISBN-10: 1985699133

Dedication

This book is dedicated to my wife and family.
Without their support and assistance,
it would not have been possible to complete this book.

About the Author

James Lawrence has been a soldier, small business owner, military advisor, and international arms dealer. He is the author of two other Pat Walsh thrillers, *Lost in Arabia* and *Arabian Vengeance*, and he currently lives and works in the Middle East.

Chapter 1

Indian Ocean

A lumbering C-130J Super Hercules plowed through the ink-black sky five thousand feet above the Laccadive Sea. The plane jostled the five passengers and four aircrew as it bounced through the choppy humid air. Standing in the cargo bay of the aircraft were five men dressed in wetsuits and wearing parachutes.

Pat Walsh did a one-eighty, turning his back to Migos, allowing him access to inspect the parachute and static line on his back. Migos slapped him on his backside to signal the okay and placed his hands on his own helmet in readiness for his own inspection. Both men wore bump helmets for this jump into the Indian Ocean, which were nothing more than foam cushions wrapped in a thin layer of plastic.

Pat began the inspection by checking the webbing on Migos's helmet and then moved methodically though a JMPI (Jump Master Parachute Inspection) checklist of common deficiencies he had memorized through endless repetition many years earlier while still a young Ranger officer.

No sooner had he finished with Migos than the white interior lights were extinguished and replaced with red lights. The cargo ramp at the tail of the aircraft began to drop. The interior of the plane was suddenly filled with the roar of wind and engine noise.

Bill Sachse, the load master, formed a hook with his index fingers and signaled for the men to attach their parachute static lines to a steel cable that ran the length of the aircraft. All five jumpers stood in a row facing the rear of the aircraft.

Pat was the closest to the tail ramp, and he was followed in order by Migos, Burnia, Jankowski and McDonald. The men held the static line cords in their left hands, with a small loop extending beyond the bottoms of their clenched fists.

Sachse left the five men and walked back towards the cargo door. Although it was obvious the ramp was open because of the noise, Pat couldn't see to the open door. His view was obstructed by a seven-and-a-half-meter rigid inflatable boat (RIB) that was propped up on a Marine Craft Aerial Delivery (MCAD) System. The heavy black rigid inflatable was resting on an aluminum sled that braced the fiberglass V-hull of the boat and kept it upright. The floor of the C-130 cargo bay had two rows of parallel steel rollers that allowed the flat aluminum base of the MCAD to roll out the cargo door with minimum resistance.

The dim glow of the red lighting gave the rail-thin Sachse a ghostlike appearance. Pat watched Sachse release the tie-downs on both sides of the MCAD, then reach on top of the RIB and retrieve a small bundle of green silk from a sealed compartment.

With his arm extended toward the open cargo door, the loadmaster opened his hand and released the tiny parachute canopy into the rushing air. The extractor parachute raced out the rear cargo door and blossomed when the cord that was anchored to the RIB played out to its full length, thirty feet behind the aircraft.

The three-ton RIB exploded into motion, rapidly picking up speed as it slid over the rollers and jettisoned into the night sky. Pat walked as fast as he could behind the MCAD, careful to stay in the center of the plane between the two sets of rollers until he too exited the aircraft.

On his way to the edge of the ramp, he watched the static line attached to the rig deploy all three cargo parachutes. He could barely see the green ChemLite attached to the RIB suspended beneath the three chutes. The cargo chute holding the sled deployed its parachute last and sped away from the slower-descending RIB.

As he exited, Pat released his static line and grabbed both sides of his reserve. He felt a strong jolt as his MC-6 steerable parachute opened, and he looked upward and confirmed that his canopy was fully deployed. He looked to his left and caught sight of the three large green canopies holding the RIB.

He pulled the left toggle and chased the RIB that was below him. It was a moonless night, and he was unable to distinguish the dark sea from the dark sky. He could smell the salty ocean. The peaceful silence was broken when he heard the loud, flat hollow crack of the RIB hull crashing into the water.

He hurriedly unclipped one side of his reserve, his waist strap and then his chest strap, leaving only two leg straps binding him to his parachute harness. He checked for the activation handle on his floatation collar, just in case. Finally he readied for impact, placing his hands on the release mechanisms of both leg straps.

Without warning, he splashed into the dark, warm waters of the Indian Ocean. He barely had time to gulp a quick breath of air before he went under. He pulled the release mechanisms on his leg straps and broke free from his harness, swimming underwater several for fast strokes to get away from his rigging and avoid entanglement with his parachute as it was absorbed into the deep ocean.

Unburdened by his harness, and with the added floatation offered by his thin neoprene wetsuit, Pat glided through the water with a powerful crawl stroke. He spotted the drifting RIB less than one hundred meters from where he had landed. He swam to the bow of the boat and pulled himself up.

Releasing the heavy risers connected to the forward parachute canopy, he began to untie the waterproof tarpaulin that sealed the interior of the boat. He untied the rigging, working in a clockwise pattern, and by the time he reached midway, he was joined by the other guys. Once all five members of the team were on board, it took only ten more minutes to ready the boat for operation.

The 258-horsepower inboard Steyr engine kicked to life on the first attempt. McDonald piloted the boat from an aluminum upright console located above the center of the hull. McDonald had radar and a FLIR system to assist in navigating through the darkness. An omnidirectional satellite system fed him the location of the target, and the GPS and an onboard computer calculated the intercept heading. The operations center in Paphos, Cyprus, sent a real-time satellite feed to a computer monitor on McDonald's console. The unlit RIB skimmed across the calm sea in total darkness at thirty knots.

Pat and the other three members of the assault team moved to the bow of the boat and opened the waterproof gear bags that were attached to the interior wall. Even in calm seas, donning dive gear at night while bouncing along at high speed is difficult. At one point, Pat almost ate his rebreather.

The movement to Kudarikilu Island took less than twenty minutes. The men wore diving masks, fins, buoyancy compensators and rebreathers on their chests. Each of the men carried suppressed HK416 assault rifles and 9mm SIG 229 pistols. The rifles were slung over the communications systems attached to the vests on their backs, and the pistols were in holsters.

Between their legs, Migos and Jankowski carried Atlas ascenders hooked to the climbing harnesses around their waists, while Pat and Burnia carried REBS Compact Launchers slung over their backs.

McDonald approached the tiny Maldives resort island from the south. He circumnavigated the tiny island, making sure to remain at least one mile offshore. As he reached the northern tip of the island, a mega yacht came into view. All five levels of the four-hundred-and-thirty-nine-foot Serena yacht were brightly illuminated. The vessel towered over the other, more modest yachts in the small harbor. The RIB stopped in the water. The four men on the assault team gave each other the thumbs-up and on Pat's signal fell backwards into the water.

As the oldest and the slowest member of the team, Pat led the underwater column of divers. He held an RJE TAC-300 navigation board in front of him with both hands as he finned the half mile to the yacht. Unable to see anything in the dark waters, he focused on the illuminated compass and depth gauge on the navigation board.

When he felt his navigation board strike the hull of the yacht twenty feet below the water line, he stopped kicking and waited for the trailing three men to catch up before slowly surfacing to check his location. He resubmerged and led the four men another fifty feet toward the direction of the bow before surfacing with the entire team.

Pat and Burnia were ten feet apart, floating on their backs with their feet pointed toward the yacht.

"How are we looking?" Pat asked McDonald over the throat mic on his radio system.

"No signs of alert. The guards at the stern dock haven't moved. The decks are clear," McDonald replied.

Burnia and Pat each held REBS launchers in their hands. Pat unhooked the cover on the rope storage box, aimed the launcher tube at the fourth level railing and pulled the trigger. The pneumatic launcher emitted a loud puff of air and sent a four-pronged titanium grappling hook and attached rope on an arc that cleared the railing sixty feet above. The hooks from both launchers sailed over the railing and landed with a thud onto the deck.

Pat and Burnia feverishly pulled down on the ropes until they were taut and firmly secured against the railing. Pat pulled the remaining line free from the launcher case and handed it to Migos. He watched Burnia do the same with Jankowski.

Migos had already discarded his fins, rebreather and mask. He expertly threaded the launcher rope connected to the grappling hook into his ascender. Holding a pistol in his right hand and the ascender remote control in his left, he toggled the push-to-talk switch on his throat mic with his left wrist.

"Ready to go, Norb?" Migos said.

"Let's go," replied Jankowski.

Migos and Jankowski depressed the up buttons on their remote controls, and the two men sped to the fourth level of the yacht with pistols at the ready. While Migos was moving, Pat discarded his dive gear, tied an end-of-the-line bowline knot to the bottom of the rope and clipped it onto the carabiner of his climbing harness. He removed an infrared ChemLite from his vest, activated it with a snap and attached it to the smooth skin of the yacht's aluminum hull with a suction cup.

"Clear," Migos whispered over his microphone.

Pat looked over at Burnia, who indicated he was set.

"Go," Pat said.

Migos and Jankowski braced the two Atlas ascenders against the rail and used them as winching devices to retrieve the other two men. Pat and Burnia were both pulled up the side of the ship at nearly the same time, with Pat only a few feet ahead. Pat climbed over the rail and unhooked the rope from the carabiner on his waist harness. The men holstered their pistols and held their rifles forward in a ready position.

The route to the VIP stateroom was an easy one. There were only two cabins on the fourth floor of the luxury cruiser. The owner's cabin, which was a luxury four-bedroom suite, and the VIP guest cabin, which was a more modest two-bedroom suite complete with a small kitchen and living room.

The yacht had been under continuous satellite surveillance ever since it had been discovered eight hours earlier by Clearwater Solutions in Paphos, Cyprus. Pat had tasked the search to his subsidiary company once he had learned his target was at sea on a vessel.

Utilizing a vast satellite network, maritime shipping network information and a proprietary artificial-intelligence-enhanced search program, Clearwater was as good as any American intelligence agency at locating people who didn't want to be found.

A real-time satellite feed was being sent to McDonald, and it was his responsibility to warn the team if the movements of any security forces were going to impede the operation.

The distance to the VIP suite required a fifty-foot walk on the outside deck and then another fifty feet through an interior hallway. The team moved in a file formation with Pat in the lead. Once they reached the door to the suite, Pat tested the door handle.

"We need to breach," Pat whispered.

Jankowski ignited the cutting rod on the Wilcox Patriot exothermic breaching system he was carrying on his back. Expertly manipulating the device with the Hellboy handset, he cut through the door's locking mechanism in less than thirty seconds.

Migos was the first one through the door, with Pat trailing behind. The two teams moved swiftly through the living room area and into a small corridor that led to the two bedrooms. Both teams held up outside the bedroom doors.

"I have movement on the top deck," reported McDonald over the radio.

"Roger," replied Pat.

The bedroom doors were unlocked. Migos and Pat entered the first bedroom while Burnia and Jankowski went into the second.

"Jackpot," Pat heard from Burnia over his comm system.

"Are we clear?" Pat asked McDonald over his radio.

"Clear," responded McDonald.

"Moving to extraction point," Pat transmitted to McDonald.

Pat and Migos moved to secure the entrance to the cabin. Burnia and Jankowski carried the prisoner by the arms. He was gagged and had flex-cuffs binding his ankles and his hands, which were cuffed behind his back. The prisoner wasn't responsive; he still hadn't recovered from being awakened by a Taser shock to his chest.

The two former CAG operators carried the medium-sized man by his arms without a hint of strain.

Pat led the team back to the ropes while McDonald, guided by the ChemLite, positioned the RIB next to the yacht and beneath the ropes for extraction. Burnia and Jankowski hooked up to the Atlas ascenders, went over the rail and positioned themselves below the railing. Pat and Burnia lifted the prisoner over the rail and handed him down to Burnia and Jankowski, who were hanging on the ropes. Burnia and Jankowski held the prisoner between them with their inside hands, and with their outside hands they grasped ascender remote controls. When Pat gave them the thumbs-up, Burnia and Jankowski descended to the RIB waiting below.

As soon as Burnia and Jankowski were off the ropes, Migos and Pat hooked the line into the carabiners of their respective climbing harnesses and abseiled down to the RIB. When both men reported clear from the rope, McDonald pushed the throttle to full, and the RIB sped away.

The trip from Kudarikilu Island to Malé was ninety miles and took almost four hours at cruising speed. The Malé International Airport was on a tiny island with a runway made from landfill that jutted out into the ocean. McDonald's position locator displayed two vehicles, the Trident C-130 and the RIB. The C-130 was on the airport tarmac inside the cargo area, parked close to the outer fence line. The display showed the RIB approaching the airport from the south.

Most commuters to the Malé International Airport arrived via boat. The airport had an extensive docking area for water ferries, which made it easy for the RIB to approach. The boat docked against the rocks only a few yards from the airport fence.

Under the cover of darkness, the four members of the assault team leapt off the RIB and moved to the fence. Burnia and Jankowski carried the prisoner. Migos cut the fence using handheld wire cutters and pulled the wire open, allowing Pat to go through first. The C-130 was parked only one hundred yards from the breach point, and the four men with prisoner in tow ran to the open cargo ramp.

Bill Sachse gave each of the men a high five as they entered the cargo hold.

"Let's get the biometrics confirmed before takeoff," Pat said.

Sachse handed Pat an iPhone, and he took a series of photos of the prisoner's face and a set of prints using a special attachment and sent them to David Forest at Clearwater. The four men stripped out of their wet suits and changed into casual civilian clothes as they waited for the response from Clearwater. After ten minutes, the phone pinged, signaling receipt of a text that said, "Faysal Ahmed Ali Al-Zharani identity confirmed."

"Who is this guy anyway?" asked Migos.

"He's a member of the Saudi royal family, a prince. At one time, he was the head of the Northeastern Oil Ministry for ISIS. Because of all the attrition, he's now the number one money man. The CIA wants him, because they think he has the contacts of whoever is left in the leadership of the organization. Plus, he also has access to the money in the accounts. That might be a reason the Saudis were treating him so well."

"Since when do the Saudis need money?" Migos asked.

"Since the price of oil dropped. They're cash-strapped these days," Pat replied.

"Why would a guy like that rate VIP guest status on a yacht owned by one of the Saudi bigwigs?" Migos said.

"That yacht is owned by the crown prince. Our prisoner is fairly close to his cousin. He's also something of an embarrassment. He wasn't just being given VIP status—he was also being hidden.

"The only reason the Agency or JSOC wouldn't do this mission is because of the political sensitivities. Getting caught assaulting the crown prince's boat would be very bad for them. For us, it's no big deal. We're deniable," Pat said.

"It's a good thing we didn't have to shoot anyone," Migos said.

"We're going to fly this guy to Bagram, and eventually he's going to wind up in Gitmo and sport an orange jumpsuit for the rest of his life. The news will report he was captured in Afghanistan, so the Saudis can save face and the US can continue to pretend the Saudi royals aren't the biggest funders and supporters of radical extremism," Pat said.

"Let's link up in Paphos next Monday. Migos, after we officially enter Maldives through the airport passport control, you and McDonald can arrange for the RIB to be shipped back to Abu Dhabi. I'm going to catch a flight back to UAE and debrief with our client," Pat said.

Chapter 2

Abu Dhabi, UAE

Pat Walsh was resting on the couch on top of the flybridge of the *Sam Houston*. The Azimut 64 yacht had been Pat's home off and on for the past five years. The Abu Dhabi Intercontinental Marina was full of similar-sized watercraft. It was early November, and the temperature was a comfortable ninety-three degrees. The annual F1 Grand Prix made Abu Dhabi a magnet for the idle rich and their playthings.

Sitting lengthwise on the couch, with the legs of his tall, lanky frame extending over the edge, Pat kept his focus on the marina walkway with the Intercontinental Hotel in the backdrop. It was early afternoon, and there was no other foot traffic except for a lone man approaching. With the sun in his eyes, Pat couldn't make out the facial features, but he could tell it was Mike Guthrie from the man's telltale limp.

Pat waved to Mike as he stepped onto the hydraulic ramp at the stern and walked onto the yacht. He lost sight of his old friend as he climbed the stairway up to the flybridge. Pat stood and gave Mike a man hug. The two men sat down across from each other on the couches surrounding the flydeck table.

"How long do you have?" asked Pat.

"I'm on the two fifteen to Dulles," replied Mike.

"How about we debrief and then have dinner? I'll get you to the airport by midnight."

Mike stood up and walked over to the refrigerator next to the gas grill, retrieving a bottle of Sam Adams Lager. He held up a second one and Pat shook his head.

"Did you finally sign up for that twelve-step program I've been recommending?" Mike asked.

"No, I'm taking it easy on the beer. I'm trying to keep up with a team of elite operators in their thirties who work out twice a day and it's freaking killing me."

Mike laughed. "Maybe it's time revert to more of a management role."

"I pretty much keep to the easier tasks and leave the heavy lifting to the studs. I've been working hard in the gym, spending a lot of time at the range and starving myself to claw back some of my old self."

"What's your assessment of the new crew?" asked Mike.

"It's a great group. Migos is proven. He's my long-standing battle buddy. He knows what I'm going to do before I do. Mark Burnia and Norb Jankowski are at a higher level than Migos and myself ever were or ever will be when it comes to operating skills. When they were in CAG, they had to have been the top assaulters. The two even look the same. Five-foot-eleven two-hundred-and-ten-pound slabs of granite. They both have a combination of power, speed and technical skills that didn't exist in my day. They're the iron fist of the team. And Roger McDonald is the person who'll take charge if I ever go down. He's the second-in-command. He's not on the same level as Migos, Burnia or Jankowski in a close fight, but he can drive anything. More importantly, he's a thinker. He's the best guy to have away from the action, looking at the bigger picture."

"What's McDonald's background?"

"He's a medic."

"You're kidding."

"It gets worse. He's a squid."

"A Navy Corpsman is your 2IC?" Mike asked incredulously.

"He's the only guy besides me over forty. A former master chief who went the Special Operations Combat Medic route. He spent a lot of time with SWCC and then with the SEAL teams. He eventually retired out of DEVGRU. I actually took him from your payroll. He was working a subcontract providing medical support at the Farm."

"It sounds like a good group. You made this last one look easy."

"It was easy. Hopefully they stay that way."

"How did you find Al-Zharani?" asked Mike.

"I used David Forrest at GSS."

"You mentioned another company called Clearwater. Who are they?" Mike said.

"I did. GSS is run out of the University of Edinburgh and it's funded by the British government. I needed to create a separate company that had all of the capabilities of GSS, but without the British oversight," said Pat.

"If you're using the same people and the same equipment as GSS, how is that going to avoid oversight by the British government?"

"It doesn't use the same equipment—that's just the thing. I replicated the architecture, hardware and everything from GSS at a facility in Paphos. I license the software from GSS. A Cray supercomputer costs less than this yacht. Clearwater is more cost-effective and more secure than using GSS," said Pat.

"I thought Forrest was a one-of-a-kind genius. How can you operate without him?"

"I can't. Forrest is part of the package. He has an ownership stake in Clearwater, and when I need him, he can either operate the system remotely from Edinburgh, or he can run it from Cyprus. He's also training one of my people to operate the system. Only Forrest and maybe a few other people in the world could build the system, but it doesn't take an Einstein to operate it," said Pat.

"You created a business just to subcontract to Trident? I doubt your mission load is going to be big enough to justify that," Mike said.

"Clearwater has a solid business plan. The company is a locator service that does nothing but find stuff, mostly ships. The sniffer AI software package that Forrest created is uncanny when it comes to tracking down ships and even smaller boats. Lloyds of London signed a five-year service contract with us already. The fact that the system can also be used to track bad guys on land or sea to support clandestine operations is just an added benefit," Pat said.

"I guess that means you're buying dinner tonight. Where are we going, anyway?"

"Asia de Cuba. It's a fusion concept on the Corniche across from the St. Regis. That release last week of the classified JFK assassination documents reminded me of how much you Langley guys love anything Cuban."

Mike shook his head. "The director decided to pass the mission to Trident once we found out Al-Zharani was in KSA. We needed some deniability in case things got ugly."

"Why is Mohammed bin Salman protecting an ISIS terrorist, anyway?" said Pat.

"MBS and Al-Zharani are second cousins. They grew up together in the same household for some unknown reason. When Al-Zharani fled Syria and returned to Saudi Arabia, he put MBS in a bad situation. Our analysts believe he exiled his childhood friend to his yacht because he didn't want him in the country. It was a temporary measure until he figured out what he was going to do with him."

"Did you get any feedback on his reaction when he found out we snatched him?"

"He didn't seem fazed by it. We think he might be grateful we solved a problem for him. He's been very forceful about cracking down on extremism. Protecting his cousin sent the wrong message. Fortunately, it was a clean operation without any collateral damage. It could have been very awkward between the two countries if the mission had gotten bloody. It was a solid plan, and your guys did a great job," Mike said.

"Have the Saudis complained or issued a protest?" asked Pat.

"No. they suspect us, of course, and they'll know it was us soon enough, but we're not going to embarrass them over this. Both sides will keep this quiet. Al-Zharani is in the detention center in Bagram. Officially, he was captured while operating in Kandahar, and he'll be transferred to Gitmo once his initial interrogation is completed."

"Is he talking?"

"He's being cooperative. Hopefully we can confiscate enough funds to cover your invoice. Even black programs have budgets. Why was the bill so high?" Mike asked.

"I had to write off all the air operations equipment we used for the boat drop. The MCAD system, including the four cargo chutes, plus the four rebreathers and five personnel rigs came to almost a million dollars. That stuff is now at the bottom of the Indian Ocean. The satellite time cost another three quarters of a million."

"I'm not quibbling over the bill. Just make sure you include the details we need to justify the expense in case of an audit."

"Fifteen million to track and confiscate God knows how many hundreds of millions in looted Iraqi Central Bank funds, plus what they took in from Iraqi oil revenues. It should be a pretty good return on investment for you guys," Pat said.

"What happens to the money is a little more complicated than that. Grabbing Al-Zharani was definitely an achievement. Up until you snagged him, he was still disbursing funds to active cells in Africa and Europe. Now we just need to keep him talking and follow the money."

Pat got up from the couch and went to the small refrigerator on the flydeck and retrieved a chilled bottle of Sassicaia He opened the bottle with a corkscrew and returned to the table with the bottle and two glasses.

"It's Italian, you should try this," said Pat.

Mike nodded, and Pat poured.

"Tell me more about how David Forrest and GSS helped you find Al-Zharani," Mike asked.

"I can't explain how his artificial intelligence system works. It's way over my head. All I know is that it's self-learning. It picks up patterns, and with complex algorithms and something called spectral sparsification, it can synthesize different intel feeds and find stuff. What makes the system work is a mystery. How it works is kind of cool. It found Zharani using open-source inputs, mostly the internet, satellites and select intrusions where appropriate."

"What's an intrusion?" Mike interrupted.

"Occasionally, the system gets hung up and the trail for the target goes cold. In those situations, we go to the last known human contact, or in one case, the CCTV cameras from the last known location, and we find the data necessary to put the system back on the trail," Pat replied.

"So, when we told you he was in KSA, you were able to track him to the yacht," Mike added.

"Exactly. And because the yacht AIS tracking system and other position-locating systems were shut off, the machine had to find the yacht using satellite searches. Once they pinpointed the location, we were able to hit the target less than eight hours later."

"That's a really good response time. Hopefully it won't be needed on your next assignment."

"I was hoping for a little downtime," Pat said. "I was planning on spending a couple of weeks in the Bahamas, and I promised the guys a break. Is this another urgent priority?"

"Yeah, it is. The sultan of Oman is near death. He has been fighting colon cancer for the last two years, and it seems he's finally lost the battle. He's in a hospital in Germany and he's in very bad shape. Once he dies, all hell is going to break loose, because the Oman secession plan is chaotic."

"What do you mean?" asked Pat.

"The al-Busaidi dynasty has ruled Oman for fourteen generations. Sultan Qaboos came to power in a coup that was backed by the British. His father, who he overthrew, was a bit of a tyrant. The sultan broke with tradition and didn't kill his dad. Instead, he exiled him to the Dorchester Hotel in London."

Mike continued, "During his forty-six-year reign, he did a lot of good in Oman. He made huge strides advancing the nation, building roads, schools, hospitals and such. He was a popular leader, but now, Qaboos is dying. He's seventy-six and single. He was married briefly to a cousin, but he never had any children. It's a pretty open secret that he was gay.

"Once he dies, the next sultan will be selected by a family council. If the council can't agree on a new monarch by majority vote within three days, then the decision reverts to the names inside two envelopes left by Qaboos," said Mike.

"Sounds like a Johnny Carson skit. Carnac the Magnificent holding an envelope to his head and saying, 'The next sultan of Oman?' Have you noticed the sultan and Carnac even wear the same headgear and dress alike?" Pat shook his head.

"Qaboos has written the name of his successor and put it in two envelopes. The first is kept in the royal palace in Muscat. The second is held in another royal palace in the southern city of Salalah. The two envelopes have the same name in them. One is just a backup."

"So far this all sounds very State Department-y. Where do I come in?" asked Pat.

"There are three frontrunners. The favorite is a cousin of the sultan, Asaad bin Tariq. Asaad is the deputy prime minister for international relations and cooperation affairs. Asaad's rivals are his two half-brothers, Haitham bin Tariq, the heritage and culture minister, and Shihab bin Tariq, a former commander of the Omani Navy. All three men are in their sixties, and it was their sister who was once married to Qaboos," explained Mike.

"I'm still not understanding where I come into this," said Pat.

"Be patient, I'm getting to that. Asaad is the status quo candidate. We expect him to continue the long-held independence policy of remaining neutral between the Iranian-led Shia and the Saudi-led Sunni influences that dominate regional foreign affairs. We believe Haitham bin Tariq will also remain neutral or possibly gravitate a little toward Saudi Arabia, policy-wise. The third cousin, Shihab bin Tariq, is much more pro-Iranian. He's the ayatollah's man in the race."

Mike continued, "When the USA signed the nuclear accord with Iran, there was a secret prisoner release that was part of the deal. The American captives were released in Oman, and the release was coordinated by Iranian intelligence through Haitham. We have enough communications intelligence to be reasonably confident that if he becomes the sultan, he will straight-arm Saudi and shift Oman to the Iranian sphere."

"The Saudis and UAE are already embargoing Qatar for making nice with Iran. If Oman goes over to the dark side, that may be enough to start a shooting war," Pat said.

"The affected parties go beyond just Iran, Saudi and UAE. China is building a city in Oman. They're constructing a free zone area in Duqm, which is about two hundred miles south of

Muscat. It's five square miles, and they've already spent ten billion dollars on what will eventually be a fifty-billion-dollar project. It'll be the only Chinese deep-water port on the Arabian Peninsula. It's a strategic port that will allow the Chinese to safeguard the flow of oil from the Strait of Hormuz to Asia. It's part of the Chinese Silk Road strategy. It's not something they will easily give up on.

"The Chinese have a heavy reliance on Arabian oil these days. Last year, they built a naval base in Djibouti that leads into the Red Sea and the Suez Canal. They just finished another deep-water base in Karachi, Pakistan, so they pretty much have the ability to block anything coming into the Arabian Gulf. Safeguarding the flow of Arabian oil is becoming a major priority for the Chinese. They buy eighty percent of Oman's oil, so the Chinese have a lot riding on who becomes the next sultan.

"The Russians also have some involvement. They're allied with Iran and Syria, which means they are very much in support of the Shia side of the sectarian divide," Mike added.

"I spend enough time in Oman to tell you that they're not very religious. The biggest religious group is the Ibadi, which are technically Sunni, but only barely. The Sunni and Shia are evenly split," Pat said.

"That's true," Mike said.

"What's the US position in all of this?" asked Pat.

"This is one of those rare occasions where we are in concert with the Chinese. We want to retain the status quo, which means Asaad."

"From how you explained it, the US could live with any of these guys," said Pat.

"We get more stability from the Chinese candidate. It's an open secret that Oman is on the verge of bankruptcy. Ever since oil prices dropped, Oman has been hemorrhaging money. If the Chinese get their candidate, they'll provide the funding needed to keep the lights on, which will make civil war a lot less likely," Mike added.

"Thanks for the lesson, although I still don't see a role for my skill set. I would think this is more of a spy-diplomat type of assignment, instead of one where you need a guy who breaks things for a living," said Pat.

"China is very active in Oman. One of the top agents from Chinese intelligence will be working from Muscat to influence the process and achieve the desired outcome. We believe since you have a close personal relationship with her, you're the best person to approach her in the spirit of cooperation," said Mike.

"Who did the Chicoms send?" asked Pat.

"Shu Xiu Wong."

"Susu? I didn't know she was that senior. I'm guessing you want me to seduce her and force her to spill the Chinese plan for world dominance," Pat said.

"You two have a history. We thought you would be the best person to approach her with an offer to share information and possibly cooperation."

"I just became very interested in this critically important assignment. I'll sail the *Sam Houston* to Muscat tomorrow. That'll provided the added advantage of weaponry, just in case," Pat said.

"Better if you don't. You're not going to be much use in an Omani prison if you get caught at customs with weapons."

"This boat has a lot of very secure hidden storage areas containing guns, ammo and tactical gear. I've been going in and out of the Port of Muscat for years without any problems. If things do get ugly and you need my team in combat mode, it'll be a lot better if they could enter the country unarmed," suggested Pat.

"Let's hope it doesn't come to that. We can probably live with any of the three cousins taking the reins. The only outcome we want is stability. The Chinese most likely think the same way."

"Who'll be my contact in Muscat?"

"Walt Berg. He'll check in with you tomorrow afternoon," Mike said.

"I'll be at the Marina Al-Bustan," Pat replied.

Chapter 3

Gulf of Oman

It had been weeks since Pat had had the *Sam Houston* out on the open water, and he was pushing the twin 1150-horsepower Caterpillar C18 engines. Seated at the helm station, which was perched fifteen feet above the water level, he checked the radar. He had his right hand on the steering wheel and his left on the two throttle controls. The thirteen-inch console screen was, for first time in the past three hours, clear of other ships.

He adjusted the range outward from the current setting of five miles to twenty and found his route clear of traffic. The Strait of Hormuz had been like rush hour on the DC Beltway, causing Pat to constantly weave around larger, slower vessels, mostly oil tankers.

It was a great day for a sail. The water was calm, with barely any wind. The sun was low off Pat's left shoulder on the port side. It was a comfortable eighty-five degrees. Pat engaged the autopilot and walked downstairs through the salon and into the galley, where he made a cup of hot green tea.

It was a little past four in the afternoon when Pat finished with customs and reached Al-Bustan Marina. He was backing the yacht into the slip, standing next to the stern console and controlling the thrusters with the joystick, when he noticed

Walt Berg walking down the slip line. Pat tossed one line to Walt and another to one of the marine attendants and then went to work connecting to external power and water.

Walt guided his thick, heavily muscled body around the tender sitting on top of the hydraulic ramp in the stern. He passed through the narrow entryway onto the yacht and stopped at his mirrored reflection on the salon door.

"Let's talk inside," Pat said as he opened the triple glass doors leading into the salon. Walt Berg was in his early forties. He was a Midwesterner, with square blond Scandinavian features. In contrast to Pat's dark sun-baked skin, Walt was pale as a ghost. He was a fireplug with wide shoulders, a thick chest and disproportionately large limbs.

"How was the trip?" Walt asked as he sat on a couch. Pat handed Walt a bottle of Sam Adams Winterfest and kept a second one for himself.

"It was a good run. I kept a cruising speed of thirty-three knots the entire trip. This boat is starting to get old, but the engines are in great shape," said Pat.

"I'm going to be your contact while you're in Oman. Officially, I'm with Commerce and Trade in case you ever need to introduce me to someone. I'll keep you up to date with any intel we have on the other players."

"Where is Susu staying?"

"She's at the Chedi," Walt said.

"That's on the north side of Muscat, isn't it?"

"Yeah, it's the closest five-star hotel to the Chinese embassy, and it's close to the royal court and the government ministries. It's a good choice."

"I expected her to be at the Ritz two miles down the road from here," Pat said.

"The Ritz is where we put most of our official delegations because it's close to the palace, but they have a major renovation going on."

"I guess I'll be staying at the Chedi, then."

"I'll give you a lift whenever you're ready."

"I plan on getting in some fishing on this trip," Pat said. "Are you interested in coming along?"

"My job is to keep an eye on you. The only thing I like more than fishing is getting paid to fish while I'm doing my job."

"Good. I'll give you a call in a couple of days."

"Have you contacted Susu yet?" asked Walt.

"She always seems to be a step ahead of me. Once I check into the hotel, most likely she'll be the one contacting me."

The drive to the Chedi took twenty-five minutes. The Chedi was a sprawling twenty-three-acre Arab-themed oceanfront resort. The lobby was a huge Bedouin tent. After check-in, the walk to Pat's ocean-view room from the lobby was a two-hundred-yard stroll through an immaculately landscaped lawn with a matrix of palm trees, gardens and fountains.

After he unpacked, Pat removed a bottle of Heineken from the minibar, opened the screen door to the porch and watched the sun set against the Indian Ocean. From his second-story balcony, he could hear the surf breaking beyond the water garden as the orange glow of the sun dipped below the horizon.

Pat finished his beer and dressed for dinner. He swapped his khaki Patagonia shorts and white Davidson College T-shirt for a pair of black pants and an untucked black button-down shirt. He made sure his Glock 19 Gen 5 and spare magazines were locked in the safe before leaving the room.

The walk to the beach restaurant was a pleasant one. The weather was still warm, with a slight breeze. The moon cast shadows from the lines of palm trees, and the soft lighting of the water gardens created islands of color in the darkness.

The beach restaurant was at the edge of the waterline. The dining room inside was large, with tall white arches and huge crystal chandeliers. An open wall led outside to a single row of tables covered by a slanted wooden porch roof held up by white columns. Red lanterns produced a subdued light barely bright enough to navigate around. Between the tables and the beach was a line of large burning gas-fired ceramic bowls.

The hostess seated Pat alone at an outside table for two. He was surrounded by couples enjoying romantic dinners. After studying the wine menu, he settled on a bottle of Domaine Leflaive 2010 chardonnay. He went through the tasting ritual and asked the wine steward to ready a second bottle. Looking out into the surf, Pat sipped his wine and imagined he was on the show *The Somm* as he struggled to identify the flavors characterizing the wine from his iPhone Vivino app.

From behind, he felt an arm wrap around his neck. Warm, smooth skin brushed lightly against the side of his face, and he felt a kiss on his cheek with the telltale scent of jasmine.

Susu slid into the seat next to him. Pat removed the wine bottle from the ice bucket, and the waitress quickly stepped in and placed another glass on the table. The two clinked glasses, and Pat reached over and took her hand. The two quietly looked out into the surf.

Pat shifted his gaze. Shu Xiu Wong was stunningly beautiful, with almond-shaped brown eyes, high cheekbones, a pretty nose and a smile that could stop traffic. She was wearing a short black dress that flattered her lithe body and gorgeous legs. At five feet seven, she barely tipped the scale at one hundred pounds and had the tiniest waist he had ever seen on a woman.

Susu signaled the waitress over, and the two conferred for several minutes while Pat worked on his second glass of wine. They started with oysters, followed by local crab soup. The main courses were wild kingfish and lobster tail. Dessert was raspberry sorbet. After Pat paid the bill, he grabbed two wineglasses and the second bottle of chardonnay with just one of his huge hands. With his other, he took Susu by the arm and led her to the beach.

The two sat in a pair of side-by-side chaise lounges positioned near the water.

"This is very romantic, Pat Walsh."

Pat poured a glass for Susu, then one for himself, and placed the bottle on the small table by his side.

"I'm glad you found me."

"You knew I would," whispered Susu as she moved over and joined Pat on his chaise lounge.

"I had a suspicion."

"You're getting too thin. I can feel your ribs."

"My work is more operational than it used to be. I've had to change things up a bit. Now I exercise, avoid loose women and drink in moderation. I'm trying to get my old body back into shape."

"Is that why you're here? Are you on an operation?" asked Susu.

"Mike Guthrie asked me to talk with you. I jumped at the chance to see you again. So, to be truthful, the real reason I'm here is to see you. Mike's request is just a pretext."

"What does Mike want?"

"He thinks the world's richest bachelor is going to check out any minute, and he expects a power struggle. He believes China and the US have a common interest in facilitating a peaceful transition with a stabilizing person on the throne. He wants me here to liaise with you and to collaborate if necessary."

"Who is the US backing?"

"The US isn't actively backing anybody. From what I've learned, we would prefer one of the cousins, with Asaad being the top choice. What we don't want is an extremist of any kind taking the throne. We don't believe such a thing would be possible without outside interference, which is where Mike thinks collaboration might be a possibility."

"That's it?" asked Susu.

"Yup."

Pat lay back on the chair, sipping his glass of chardonnay, and Susu moved onto his lap and kissed him. Pat tried to put his glass on the side table and accidentally knocked the wine bottle into the sand.

"I hope that wasn't expensive wine." She smiled.

"I'm just glad it didn't break." Pat wrapped Susu in his arms.

He woke the next morning with Susu's body next to him, clinging forcefully to him with her arms around his neck. He was lying on his left side, and he moved his right hand from the crown of her head down through her long black hair to the base of her back, then to her beautifully shaped derriere.

"You're restless. Where are you going?" asked Susu in a whisper.

"They have a hundred-meter pool. I was planning on swimming and then going to do some work on my boat," Pat replied.

"Stay with me a little longer."

"Convince me."

Susu moved her hand.

"Okay."

"What else are you going to do today?" she asked.

"After I'm finished on the *Sam Houston*, I was planning to hit the gym and then maybe get a massage at the spa."

"How do you still have the energy to work out twice?" whispered Susu.

"We can stay here all day if that's what you want," said Pat.

"I have to go in a little while." Susu squeezed him in her arms. Pat rolled over onto his back, and Susu rested her head on his chest.

"Are you okay?" asked Susu.

"Not really. I have no idea if I'll ever be with you again. These trysts leave me more unsatisfied every time."

"You've brought this up before. Are you willing to live in China?" asked Susu.

"I told you I was, ages ago."

"Once I retire, the Chinese government will never again allow me to leave China," said Susu.

"There are lots of nice places in China, and as long as I can still leave when I want, that's not a problem for me."

"You will have to retire too."

"That'll be a lot easier than you think."

"Where will we live?" asked Susu.

"If it's up to me, I vote Hainan Island in the South China Sea. The surfing is legendary."

"Are you sure you want to grow old with me? Your preferences have always been for much younger girls. What happened to that twenty-something surfer girl?" asked Susu.

"She dumped me."

"Why?"

"The more she learned about my past and what I do for a living, the less she liked me."

Susu kissed Pat. "I'm sorry."

"No, you're not. Surfer girls believe in karmic retribution and that kind of stuff. We were never a good match."

"Your past doesn't scare me."

"Nothing scares Mata Hari, and you know as much about my past as I do. We were made for each other. It's time you stopped resisting and being so coy and annoying and simply accepted that fact," Pat said.

"You and I should be together, eternal mates," said Susu in a questioning tone.

"We always have been. I can't believe it's taken you so long to figure that out. I've been after you for years."

"And you've had a lot of girlfriends in that time."

"Poor substitutes. Desperate attempts to salvage my damaged self-esteem because you rejected me."

"What should I do?" asked Susu.

"Be a good girl and do as you are told."

"Maybe I don't love you." Susu pouted.

"I don't believe that."

"I reach mandatory retirement at the end of this year. When I do, you'll join me in Hainan," said Susu with a grin.

"I'll start looking for a beach house today."

"Try to keep it modest."

"Of course."

"I don't believe that."

"You shouldn't."

"Let's have dinner tonight on the boat. I'll cook for you."

"I can't. I have to work late."

"Take a room key and meet me here when you're done."

"I'll try. No promises."

"Feel free to surprise me."

Chapter 4

Marib, Yemen

Colonel Morteza Hosseinpour-Shalmani strained under the heavy burden of his backpack. The nylon straps cut into his shoulders, and his shirt was soaked with sweat. A blanket of clouds blocked the night sky, preventing even the tiniest sliver of moonlight from penetrating them.

It was increasingly difficult for Shalmani to find his footing on the treacherous mountain trail. He raised his right hand and signaled for the two men following him to stop. Removing a Russian handheld thermal viewer from his rucksack, he turned it on and gave it a few seconds to cool, then scanned the desert valley below him.

To his west, he could see the village of Nuqub, whose structures showed black-hot through his optics. The village had at one time been home to more than a thousand inhabitants, but the villagers had all been killed or run off after a series of Saudi air strikes many months earlier. Now all that remained was dozens of badly damaged brick structures and a combat outpost manned by a platoon of Saudi infantry equipped with four 4x4 MATV armored vehicles, each with a mounted 12.7mm machine gun on the top. Joining the Saudis were a company of Yemeni dismounted infantry forces, whose number Shalmani estimated to be between eighty to one hundred.

He removed the thermals and scanned with his naked eye to the east, where the valley widened into flat desert. He could just barely detect the lights from the coalition forward operating base in the city of Marib. FOB Safer was a huge walled compound that was home to thousands of Saudi, Emirati, Sudanese and Yemeni troops. It had been established as a major base of operations to position forces to seize the capital city of Sana'a, located eighty miles to the west. One of the greater Houthi victories earlier in the conflict had been a successful missile attack that had killed and wounded more than seventy Emirati soldiers at the FOB.

Coalition efforts to seize Sana'a had been stalemated for almost a year. The ring of combat outposts (COPS) around FOB Safer represented the limit of advance. The coalition forces had learned the hard way that venturing beyond the COPS into the narrow mountain passes was a surefire way to get ambushed. The FOB was supplied by road from the north by Saudi Arabia. It also had a serviceable airfield capable of landing C-17 aircraft, and it had a contingent of attack and utility helicopters.

The handheld thermals only had a range of five kilometers. From his perch a mile above the valley floor, that was all he would need to observe and direct the movement of his forces against the enemy. He had been conducting reconnaissance for tonight's objective for many weeks. FOB Safer was ringed by eight combat outposts. He had chosen the COP at Nuqub to attack because it was the only one he could find defended by Saudis. He knew for his plan to work, the force he attacked had to be composed of either Saudi or Emirati troops. The coalition leadership would likely not expend precious resources to rescue a Sudanese or Yemeni unit.

After he'd found his target, he next had to wait for the ideal weather conditions. A heavy cloud ceiling below one thousand feet was essential to minimize the threat of detection by unmanned aerial vehicles (UAV). A low cloud cover would also restrict the dreaded enemy air force's ability to provide close air support, leaving only artillery and attack helicopters for him to deal with.

Once his plan had been crafted, he'd had to wait a full month for the right weather conditions. Since it only rains nine days a year in the Sana'a region of Yemen, the cloud cover his plan needed was a rarity.

Colonel Shalmani's force consisted of forty-one Houthi fighters along with his own detachment of eight Iranian Revolutionary Guard commandos, called Quds. He had great faith in his men. Most had been with him for the better part of a decade. They had fought with him against the Americans in Iraq, and later when he had battled ISIS and the rebel forces in Syria. Every one of his men was a seasoned combat veteran. The Quds were responsible for killing more than four hundred Americans in Iraq. He was one of the Quds who had brought the enhanced penetrating IEDs to Iraq and had shown the anti-American Shia fighters how to use them. The deployment of his team and the dozens of similar Quds detachments to Yemen had yielded similar results. To date, his team's greatest achievement was the destruction of an Emirati Baynunah-class frigate with a surface-to-surface missile fired from the shore. Colonel Shalmani eagerly anticipated matching that earlier accomplishment tonight.

It was not until after two in the morning that all of his units reported being in position. The men had rehearsed the attack more than twenty times over the past three days. He was confident they would execute the plan to perfection.

He picked up the radio microphone and depressed the Send key. In a calm voice, he said, "Fire the mortars."

Moments later, he heard the distinctive thud of 82mm mortars firing in the distance. He mentally ticked off the time of flight, and less than thirty seconds later, he watched the mortar rounds impact inside the walls of the village. Six bright orange flashes lit up the village landscape. It took another ten seconds for the sound of the explosions to reach his ears. The six mortar tubes were behind the hills, out of sight. The mortars maintained a steady barrage on the objective, each tube firing a round every ten to fifteen seconds.

After confirming his indirect fires were on target, he picked up the radio handset. "Support Team, engage."

Immediately, green tracers from the support position began to pepper the village. The 7.62mm PKM machine guns could be seen through his thermals at the base of the valley west of the village. The machine gunners were only six hundred meters from Nuqub, and Colonel Shalmani watched several of the Yemenis soldiers defending the village fall to the withering fire. Red tracers from the heavy MATV 12.7mm machines guns began to hit in the general area of the support position as the Saudis began to return fire.

"Assault Team, move," Colonel Shalmani ordered. From his observation position, he watched a force of twenty-five Houthis rise from the shallow wadi north of the support position and slowly advance toward the village. Salvos of Saudi artillery began to explode behind the advancing infantry.

The 155mm high-explosive rounds were off target and too far behind the assault force to do any harm, and the advance of the assault force was purposely slow. It was a feint, not a genuine attack against the numerically superior force. The purpose of the operation was not to overrun the combat outpost, but instead to force the Saudis to commit the quick reaction force.

When the attack had been ongoing for twenty-five minutes, Colonel Shalmani grew concerned that his mortar men and machine gunners would run out of ammunition. Through his optics, he saw several of his Houthi assault team members sprawled on the ground, either dead or wounded. The support position must have also taken casualties, because he could hear only four machine guns still engaging the village. After a quick sweep of the situation below him, he returned his attention to the east, toward FOB Safer.

The mortar fire ebbed as some of the crews began to run out of ammunition. He chastised himself for not checking the individual loads, since if some crews were already dry, it could only mean the rounds had been unevenly distributed.

The assault team had halted its advance less than two hundred meters from the village. The men were taking cover behind a small embankment, occasionally popping up to engage the defenders with their AK-47s. Either the PKM machine guns from the support position were slowly being destroyed, or they were running out of ammunition. Green tracer fire could only be seen coming from two positions.

Despite the cool night air, Colonel Shalmani began to sweat. He desperately scanned the horizon to the east, and a wave of relief washed over him when he heard the distinct beat of rotor blades in the air between breaks in the cacophony of the battle below. Vectoring his thermals onto the growing sound, he was able to see the black-hot thermal signatures of two Apache Longbow Helicopters as they approached the village. The two gunships were five hundred feet apart, moving abreast at an altitude of five hundred feet.

From the black darkness of the desert floor, two orange streaks shot up into the sky. The colonel watched both aircraft bank in opposite directions in an effort to evade the SAMs while a flurry of red flares shot out from underneath each aircraft. The evasive maneuvers and IR countermeasures saved one Apache, but the one to Colonel Shalmani's left exploded into a huge fireball. The six Quds team members lying in ambush on the desert valley floor fired a second volley of SA-14s at the remaining aircraft as it was still banking in a high-g turn. More IR countermeasures erupted from the Apache. This time, both missiles found the target, and the aircraft spun wildly out of control into the village, where it crashed into a building and exploded in a huge fireball.

With the Saudis distracted by the destruction of their quick reaction force, the remnants of the assault force were able to advance the remaining two hundred meters to the perimeter of the COP. From the outer walls of the village, the Houthi assault force rained RPG-7 fire at the Saudi armored vehicles, managing to set one on fire.

After witnessing the destruction of the Apaches and the deaths of their compatriots in the MATV, the Saudis had seen enough. The remaining three MATVs backed out of their forward battle positions and raced out of the village on the east road toward the safety of FOB Safer.

Looking down from his perch, Colonel Shalmani scanned to the burning hulk of the second Apache hit on the north side of the village. Moving his thermals to the right, he could see the black-hot flames of the first Apache, which had gone down two kilometers east of the village. Finally, he scanned back to the left in time to see three MATVs moving fast as they broke free from the cover of the village and entered the open desert.

The same Quds commandos that had destroyed the Apaches were lying in ambush parallel to the road, waiting for the Saudi vehicles. Earlier, they had emplaced a line of TM-72 Russian mines on the only road leading back to the FOB. Each commando held an extended RPG-75M in his hand as he lay prone on his belly.

The fleeing MATVs traveled in a column at a speed of fifty miles per hour with headlights switched on. The lead vehicle noticed the surface-laid mines too late, and the driver hit the brakes and skidded into the tilt rod of a land mine. The blast penetrated the vehicle's belly plate, instantly killing all four men inside. The two trail MATVs skidded to a stop before the minefield and blindly sprayed 12.7mm heavy machine gun fire in every direction. The tracers from the panicked gunners went over the heads of the unseen ambushers, who remained prone less than one hundred meters from the Saudi vehicles.

The first salvo of 66mm antitank rockets hit both vehicles on the flank. A door to one of the vehicles opened and several soldiers spilled out. Seconds later, both MATVs exploded from hits by the second salvo of RPGs. The Quds detachment stood from their ambush line and approached the burning vehicles with AK-74s drawn.

"Initiate exfiltration," Colonel Shalmani ordered from his perch. He watched as the surviving Yemeni assault team members withdrew from the edge of the village and started back to the cover of the wadi and the support team headed back to the cover of the hills with casualties in tow.

"Why aren't you moving?" Colonel Shalmani shouted to his Quds detachment ambushers.

"We have three Saudi prisoners. One of them is an officer," replied the team leader.

"Kill the enlisted. Make an example of the officer before you cut his throat. Be sure you film it. We'll give the Saudi cowards something to think about the next time they consider venturing from the protection of their base."

He stood, returned his rucksack to his back and began the descent from his observation point. The sting of the rucksack straps on his shoulders was eased by the thought of the Saudi officer being raped, tortured and killed below.

By dawn the next morning, Colonel Shalmani and his men were ensconced in the protection of a mountain cave. Radio and cell phone signals were heavily monitored in the area. Communications with command were accomplished through a high-burst satellite communication system set up at the entrance to the cave. The team sent only one message per day to the headquarters in Tehran.

Today's ops report was notable because after it was sent, they received a reply. "Prepare for exfil. You're being recalled to Tehran."

Chapter 5

Muscat, Oman

At dawn, Pat parked his rented Ford Explorer at the Al-Bustan Marina. When he arrived at the *Sam Houston*, Walt Berg was already standing on the narrow wooden walkway next to the yacht. Pat retrieved a fishing rod and an empty five-gallon plastic bucket from storage and walked Walt to the end of the slipway.

"Been waiting long?" Pat asked.

"About thirty minutes. I didn't want to be late. I've been looking forward to this trip for days."

"Let's hope the fish are biting," Pat said as they reached the end of the slip furthest from the shore.

"The amount of sea life in this water is amazing," Walt said. The two men looked down into the water.

"Drop the line five feet below the surface, and don't pull it up until you have a fish on all five hooks. We'll only need about twenty for live bait, so don't try to fill the entire bucket," said Pat.

"They'll hit on just shiners?"

"Yeah, they just jump right on. You'll spend more time pulling them off the hook than getting them on. The best size is around six inches. Anything below four, just throw back. I'll prep the boat while you get us something to fish with."

Walt returned to the boat twenty minutes later with a heavy bucket, which Pat secured at the back end of the stern before the lines. He then joined Walt on the flydeck, where he took the controls at the helm and went underway.

"The conditions are good. We should get a little chop once we get out a few miles. Our destination is forty miles offshore, and it's going to take an hour and fifteen minutes to get there. There's fresh coffee in the galley, and if you're hungry, its fully stocked," Pat offered.

Once the *Sam Houston* had moved beyond the marina navigation markers, Pat eased the throttles forward until the speed reached thirty knots.

Walt returned with two coffee cups.

"Walking up a flight of stairs balancing those cups is no small feat. You're a legitimate sailor," Pat said.

"I almost did a header when you goosed the accelerator," Walt replied.

"I'll try to be gentler in the future."

"How about we talk shop now, so when we get to the fishing spot, we can concentrate on enjoying ourselves?" Walt said.

"You want me to go first?"

Walt removed a leather notebook from a bag he had left on the flybridge table. "Please."

"I met Susu for dinner three nights ago and passed her Mike's message. She was amenable to the idea but had to talk with her management before officially responding. I met her again last night, late. She came to my room at around midnight. She let me know that her bosses okayed some info sharing and the possibility of further coordination."

"Is that it?"

"Yeah."

"How are things between you and Susu?"

"Better than they've ever been."

"You shouldn't get too close to her."

"I'm just a glorified liaison officer. If Chinese intel has something they want the CIA to know, Susu will pass it to me. If you have info you want the Chinese to know, I'll pass it to Susu. Everything else between Susu and myself is personal."

"That's not how it works. We need you to collect as much information as possible on what she's up to. It might prove useful."

"I'm an operator, not an agent. I'm sure you have a whole bunch of highly trained professionals working this situation. If a problem does present itself that requires my skill set, I'm on standby. But I'm going to leave the spying stuff to the pros," Pat said.

"We don't have a lot of agents on this. Oman has never been a regional priority. There's too much going on in Iraq and Syria. Saudi Arabia is a huge concern at the moment. MBS has launched a preemptive countercoup. He's threatening war with Lebanon, and now it looks like the king is about to step aside and allow MBS to ascend to the throne. Yemen is draining a lot of our resources, and there's a strong chance of another shooting war between Israel and Lebanon. We'll take any help we can get," said Walt.

"I'm just here to pass info back and forth between Susu and the Agency. I have my team ready to insert if you need muscle, but the spooky spy-versus-spy stuff is not my forte, believe me."

"Forget I asked."

"Any news on the sultan?"

"No change."

"Does Asaad still look good as his successor?"

"We think so. He seems to as well. He's beefed up his security detail, and if the flow of ministers to his offices is any indicator, the senior members of the Omani government are equally convinced."

"Anything you want me to communicate to the Chinese?" Pat asked.

"Most of the chatter we're picking up is coming from the Iranians and Saudis. We're most concerned about the Iranians. If the Chinese have any indication of what the Iranians are up to, that would be helpful."

"Consider it done."

Six hours later, the two men both stood on the hydraulic platform at the back end of the stern. Walt's arms strained under the weight of what looked to be the biggest fish of the day. The heavy-duty graphite rod was bent like a question mark, and Pat held the gaff with both hands, waiting for the fish to come within his range. Pat glanced over to Walt and saw his excitement through the heavy mask of white sunscreen covering his face.

"You know, that grin and that white face paint make you look like the clown in that Stephen King movie," Pat said. Walt did not respond; his concentration was absolute.

The big fish made one last attempt to run, and when tension from the heavy line forced it to circle back toward the boat, Pat swung the hook and snagged it with the gaff. The fish was more than three feet long, and as he pulled it out of the water, he realized it must have weighed at least forty pounds.

"Let me get my phone so I can take a picture."

"Use my phone. This fish is a monster. This is unbelievable," Walt replied.

"You may want to wipe some of that sunblock off your face. This is a shot that you're going to want to keep."

"What are we going to do with all these fish?" Walt asked as he cradled the enormous fish in both arms while Pat snapped pictures.

"When we get back to the marina, I'll send one to the Blue Marlin. They'll make it the nightly special, and that's where I plan on eating dinner tonight."

"You should take the other three home. The staff at the marina will clean and pack them up for you."

"I wish I could join you for dinner, but I need to get back."

"Susu is meeting me at seven. I didn't think you would be able to stick around. I'm sure you have to file a report as soon as we get back."

Pat spent the next three hours working on the boat. The list of maintenance and cleaning tasks was never-ending and always gave him something to do. At six thirty, he went downstairs to the owner's cabin to shower. When he emerged from the bathroom, he found Susu sitting at the small table across from the bed.

Susu got up from her seat and wrapped her arms around his neck, giving him a long kiss.

"How was fishing?"

"It was awesome. We hooked four good-sized yellowtail."

"Is that what we're having for dinner?"

"I strongly recommend it. The chef at the Blue Marlin does a great job with tuna."

"What are your plans?"

"Let's eat and then go for a night cruise."

"That sounds romantic."

"It is. The weather is perfect. We can lay out on the sundeck on the bow. In the morning, we can watch the sunrise. The rocky cliffs along the shoreline, the sea and the sunrise together are spectacular."

"You want me to sleep outside, on the deck?"

"It's very comfortable. The sundeck has a very comfortable cushion. This is a high-end Italian custom-designed yacht. We're not talking about the bed of a pickup truck here or a rickshaw or whatever you guys used during your youthful dating days."

After dinner Pat and Susu returned to the *Sam Houston*, it took only thirty minutes to position the boat five miles offshore and fifteen miles south of the marina. The water was too deep to use the anchor, so Pat engaged the positioning system to maintain location against the drift using the GPS and the thrusters.

"Well, what do you think of this spot?" asked Pat.

"The stars are amazing."

"There's no ambient light at all. You can see every star in the sky."

"This was a good idea."

"Tomorrow morning, the shoreline will come into view. It's three hundred feet of vertical cliffs. This is one of the most beautiful spots in the world."

"What are we going to do until dawn?" asked Susu.

"I have some ideas." Pat wrapped the blanket around her and lowered her onto the sundeck.

Later, Pat and Susu were sitting up, propped up by pillows under the blanket and drinking wine.

"Did your CIA contact have anything useful to report?" asked Susu.

"Not really. He made it clear that Oman is very much a sideshow in the region. The US is much more concerned about what's going on in the conflict zones and in Saudi. He wants to know what China thinks is going to happen, and he's especially interested in what you think Iran is up to."

Susu took a sip of her wine and paused as if she were pondering the question. "Once the anticorruption arrests are completed and all of the senior military and royal family members suspected of not being loyal to MBS are imprisoned, King Salman is going to abdicate."

"CIA has the same opinion."

"We believe Iran is going to take action in Lebanon and Oman to weaken Saudi and attempt to throw them into a civil war during MBS's transition as king."

"How?" asked Pat.

"MBS withdrew Prime Minister Hariri from Lebanon and forced him to resign. The Lebanese government is Hezbollah-controlled, with Hariri being the only voice for the Sunni. MBS announced last month that a state of war exists between Saudi and Lebanon. Hezbollah has accelerated the stockpiling of rockets in Lebanon. They have more than one hundred and fifty thousand aimed at Israel. We believe Hezbollah, under the direction of Iran, is going to launch a major rocket attack against Israel during the MBS transition period, which we are now in. Facing an onslaught of thousands of rockets, Israel will have no choice but to retaliate and repeat the invasion of 2006."

"How does Israel invading Lebanon help the Iranians?"

"MBS is recognized as an ally of Israel. The king actually visited Tel Aviv last month. Hezbollah's rockets could overwhelm the Iron Dome system and inflict heavy casualties on the civilian population. If that happens, it's likely Israel will retaliate in force. When Israel launches a full-scale invasion into Lebanon, it's going to cause thousands of Lebanese casualties. The humanitarian cost to all sects within Lebanon will be horrific, which will inflame the Sunni and Shia populations and open an even bigger rift between MBS's government and the religious extremists in Saudi."

"That's a pretty complicated scenario, but I guess it could work that way."

"MBS's popularity among the Saudi people will shrink because the Wahhabis consider him an ally of Israel and an enemy of Lebanon. Israel was defeated in 2006 when they invaded Lebanon. The Israelis didn't have the will to cause the number of civilian casualties required for tactical success. This next time, they'll have no choice. They'll have to destroy those rockets, and the humanitarian cost to accomplish that will be brutal. Iran is counting on Israeli brutality fueling anti-Israel sentiment—and by association, anti-MBS sentiment—among his people. MBS has made a lot of enemies with his anticorruption campaign; many members of the royal family would jump at the opportunity to take him out," Susu added.

"Where does Oman fit into all of this?" asked Pat.

"The Saudis have been defeated at every turn by Iran. Saudis backed the Syrian rebels who have been destroyed, leaving Assad and Syria as an Iranian puppet. Iran is weakening Saudi with a proxy war in Yemen that's not going well for the Saudis. The failure to defeat the Houthis is a humiliation for MBS, who is the architect of that war. Iran has gained control of Iraq and Lebanon, where their terrorist arm, Hezbollah, has become the dominant political party. Qatar has been embargoed by Saudi, which has moved Qatar closer to the Iranian sphere in yet another setback for MBS. If the next sultan of Oman turns his back on Saudi and is pro-Iranian, that's going to give Tehran yet another victory."

"These are desperate times for Saudi Arabia. The losses are piling up," Pat added.

"Saudi has to change, or they'll perish. We believe the moderate form of Islam and the anticorruption reforms undertaken by MBS are essential to the survival of Saudi Arabia. Saudi stability is important to China because oil is critical to our economy. We don't buy a lot of oil from Saudi, but if they get disrupted, it will affect the entire market, including us. China will not allow Iranian domination of this region. We intend to stop them in Oman, and we hope the US has the same position," she said.

"I'm pretty sure that's the case, but I'll get back to you with official confirmation from Mike on that. What we had previously discussed is that any of the three cousins would be okay with the US. Is that your position?"

"No, it isn't. We will accept either Asaad or Haitham, but not Shihab. He's controlled by the Iranians, and he would be a disaster," answered Susu.

"Shihab's a long shot. Based on what you told me, the only way he's going to get the job is if the Iranians do something nefarious," Pat said.

"The reason I'm here is because we expect the Iranians to try something, as you say, nefarious. So far, our actions have been limited—it's been just an influence and information campaign—but the possibility does exist for stronger measures."

"I thought you were here for me."

"Unfortunately, I'm not going to be able to spend as much time with you. I have work. Things are picking up," said Susu.

"China can have your days, I'll settle for the nights. How about you agree to stay with me every night until Arab Liberace bites the dust? After that, you can devote yourself full-time to China," Pat said as he wrapped his arms around Susu.

"No," replied Susu, and Pat rolled onto his back away from her.

"All this China, China, China talk is getting annoying. The only thing worse is the depressing situation in the Middle East. It's time to step away and make more time for me."

"You're very distracting. I need to focus."

"I'm providing a vital intelligence channel. You should consider these overnights as your duty. Think of your country. Maybe you should be like a proper British girl during Victorian times—close your eyes and think of England."

"The problem is I can't do my job when I'm around you."

"So, after this boat trip, you're moving out?" asked Pat.

"Yes, but only until this assignment is over, and then together, we'll move to Hainan," Susu replied as she hugged Pat.

"I guess I can deal with that," Pat said as he removed the quilted blanket covering Susu.

Chapter 6

Muscat, Oman

Pat sat on the flybridge and watched Susu navigate the narrow marina walkway on her way to a waiting black Audi A8. He snatched a pair of binoculars from the helm station and watched her disappear into the car. The window rolled down and he saw Susu blow him a kiss, which made him smile and feel a little less sorry for himself.

With very little work to do, he decided to occupy himself with his first-ever Oman surfing experience. He ran down from the flybridge and untied the boat and then set a heading for Masirah Island. During the Second Gulf War, Masirah had been used as an air base for missions into Iraq. Pat remembered at the time it was called Camp Justice, although he had never actually visited. His old unit had staged out of Doha for the initial invasion. Masirah held a small place in Special Operations history because it was used during the Desert One mission in the failed attempt to rescue the Iranian hostages in 1979.

It was almost two in the afternoon when Pat anchored off the coast of Surf Beach in the southern part of the island. Half a mile from shore, the cobalt water was a shallow thirty feet. The wind was a steady twenty miles an hour from the east and the temperature was a humid eighty degrees. Masirah island was ninety-five miles long and had a population of twelve thousand. Most areas of the island were deserted. The island could only be reached by ferry and was too far out of the way to attract many tourists.

From the flybridge, Pat scouted the beach with his binoculars. He saw two sea turtles on the rocky shore and several birds; otherwise, the beach was empty. He ran downstairs to the crew quarters, where he kept his gear, and emerged with his surfboard and a full wetsuit, complete with neoprene boots to protect him from the sharp rocks.

The swells were six feet in height and breaking to the right. The surf was consistent, and after the second run, Pat was able to make the most of them. The sun was beginning to set when he found his last swell. He felt the burning in his shoulders as he paddled furiously with his powerful arms to propel the eight-foot board into the wave. He popped up to a crouch as soon as he felt the board drop, and then he started to carve a series of lazy S turns. When the wave began to break, he banked hard to the left and popped up over the wave before falling. He crawled onto his board, pointed it toward the open ocean and started to paddle back to the *Sam Houston*.

Drinking an ice-cold bottle of Sam Adams to clear the salty taste from his throat, Pat set the autopilot from the main wheelhouse and then headed downstairs to his cabin for a quick shower. As the yacht steered itself back to Muscat, he grilled a thick New Zealand rib eye with asparagus on the side and helped himself to several more beers. Afterward, Pat set the Raymarine radar so it would sound an alarm if another vessel came within five miles of his boat, then lay out on the galley bench chair behind the helm station and went to sleep.

The next morning, Pat returned to his slip at the Al-Bustan Marina rested, refreshed and a little sore from the previous day's exercise. He was connecting the power and water when he saw Walt Berg's black Chevy Tahoe pull into a parking space near his yacht. Expecting only Walt, he was surprised to see Mike Guthrie emerge from the passenger side of the SUV.

The men shook hands on the slipway, and then all three retreated to the main salon of the *Sam Houston*. The salon had three cream-colored leather couches connected in a horseshoe array across from a retractable big-screen television. Pat poured coffee, and each of the three men sat on a couch around a coffee table.

"I have the NFL package on satellite if either of you wants to catch up on any of yesterday's games," Pat said.

"Put the Skins game on. I missed it because of the flight, and I haven't checked the scores yet," Mike said.

After a few minutes with the controls of the satellite, TV and Apple TV, Pat was able to get the kickoff of the archived Cowboys and Redskins game.

"Do you want to put a bet on your native American cultural appropriators, Mike?" asked Pat.

"If you're betting, that must mean you already know the score. Thanks for ruining it."

"No, I don't know the score, honest. If you guys are hungry, I can order out at the Blue Marlin, and in case you've forgotten—and this is a key selling point—they have real pork bacon and not the veal stuff."

"That sounds good, thanks," Mike said while Walt nodded.

It wasn't until the fourth quarter, when the Redskins were up 38-7, that the conversation turned to work.

"Anything new from Susu?" asked Mike.

"I told her that any of the three cousins would be acceptable to the US. She was firm that Shihab wouldn't be acceptable to China," Pat said.

"Did she give any indications of how they would react if Shihab was selected by the family council?" Mike asked.

"No, but she was firm. Which I took to mean they would influence things the Chinese way. They want Asaad. I'm fairly sure that any family member who is part of the council voting for Asaad is going to receive a gift from the Chinese government."

"What do you think will happen to any council member who doesn't vote for Asaad?" asked Mike.

"If they vote for Haitham, I think they'll be okay, but if they vote for Shihab, then I'm sure they'll be warned that bad things could happen to them," Pat said.

"What kind of bad things?" Mike asked.

"Economic. Members of the council are wealthy, but none are billionaires like Asaad. They're all vulnerable because they fall into that category of being rich enough to have a lot to lose, but not rich enough to be impervious to being wiped out by a well-funded adversary. Susu is calling the shots, and she'll know what levers to pull," Pat said.

"Do you think the Chinese will get Asaad crowned?" asked Mike.

"There are other forces in play. The Iranians, Russians, Brits, and us, of course. The Chinese and the Iranians seem to be the most committed to influencing the outcome. Of the two, I would put my money on the Chinese candidate."

"Has she turned you yet? Have you joined the Communist Party?" Mike asked.

"I'm still going through the background check. I'm worried they'll find out I'm a greedy capitalist and discover I'm only interested in joining for the girls."

"Is that all you have?"

"I already sent you the summary of what she said about the Iranians' intentions and how she believes they're up to something. Including the bit about the Lebanon tie-in."

"At Langley, they don't believe Hezbollah is preparing to launch an attack on Israel. We saw what they did in the run-up last time, and the indicators aren't there, yet, anyway. Even though the Lebanese were able to stop the last invasion, they paid a heavy price for it. Hezbollah has lost a lot of fighters in Syria over the past two years. They're war-weary. We don't think they have the appetite to take on Israel at the moment."

"I hope your analysts are right and the Chinese are wrong. Anyway, this has been an easy assignment, and I'm not complaining, but how much longer is this going to take?"

"A couple of weeks at most. Sultan Qaboos is in very bad shape."

"Are you sticking around for the duration?"

"I head back to Washington tonight."

***

Having to react to an impending radar alarm all night prevented Pat from getting quality sleep. The surfing, the all-night sail and the heavy breakfast were making it difficult for him to keep his eyes open. He was grateful when Mike and Walt left. Minutes later, he was sound asleep in his cabin.

When Pat awoke it was to Susu's touch. Although it was still daylight, the portholes were covered and the cabin was completely dark. Susu had entered the cabin, disrobed and slipped under the covers without waking Pat. It wasn't until he felt the gentle touch of her fingertips on his chest that he woke up. He opened his eyes, but it was too dark to see; he recognized her by her smell. When his hands found her tiny waist, it removed all doubt. Without speaking, the two joined bodies.

When the two finally got out of bed, it was already dark outside. Susu went to the galley and began to prepare dinner.

"What are you making?" asked Pat.

"Chicken stir fry. You must love Asian food. You have everything I need."

"I do. I've never seen this domestic side of you. I like it. Do you want some help?"

"You can pour some wine, and then I need to update you on some developments."

Pat went to the wine cooler in the salon and removed a bottle of chilled Chateau Ste. Michelle chardonnay. He poured two glasses and handed one to Susu, who took a sip, then put the glass down and returned to the task of chopping vegetables. Pat sat down on the bench chair at the galley table and watched Susu work from behind. She wore a short green silk bathrobe, and her hair was in a ponytail.

"Sultan Qaboos died this morning," she said.

"I've been checking my phone for news. There's nothing on the internet about it."

"They'll keep his death a secret until they've decided on his replacement. Too risky otherwise."

"Has the family council convened?"

"Yes, they're meeting at the palace in Bustan."

"That's practically next door to us."

"Which explains my being in the neighborhood."

"Are the three cousins at the palace?"

"Yes. Once the family makes a decision, they'll announce the death of Qaboos and the name of the new sultan."

"How confident are you the family will elect Asaad?"

"Very."

"Will you be staying with me until they make an announcement?"

"No, I have to leave after dinner. I have an appointment."

"How long do you think it'll take for the announcement?"

"Two, maybe three days."

"What's going to happen with Iran when Asaad becomes sultan?"

"What do you mean?"

"Iran is Oman's biggest trading partner. Will Asaad change that?"

"No. I've had many discussions personally with Asaad; he'll continue Qaboos's policies. He will continue to allow Qatar to utilize its waterways and circumvent the Saudi/UAE embargo. The Iranian natural gas pipeline construction will go on, and he will stay out of the Yemeni conflict. On the other hand, the three US bases will remain in Oman, and our port development project in Duqm will continue. Asaad is the best choice for all parties concerned."

"Two days of interfamily negotiations dividing up the estate, followed by a coronation and a national funeral. We should be out of here and onto better and brighter things by next week."

"How is the real estate shopping going?"

"I've contacted an agent. It's a complicated market. We need to visit. Hainan has two hundred small islands. It's going to take time to find the right place. I think we should sail to Hainan and then island-hop until we find our Xanadu."

"That sounds like a great idea."

Susu left after dinner, and Pat began making preparations to sail to Hainan. He used a chart-plotting software program that calculated the best route based on his cruising speed and range. The trip was 2,884 nautical miles, which mandated a stop midway for fuel. Singapore looked to be the most likely waypoint.

Logistics and route planning consumed Pat for the next six hours. What he loved about sailing was also what he enjoyed most about military operations—the challenge of identifying a complex problem and developing a plan to solve that problem and then the satisfaction of executing the plan successfully.

The past week in Muscat had been nice, because he had gotten to spend time with Susu, but he was starting to find the waiting game boring. It was nice to have an end in sight.

Exploring the South China Sea with Susu excited him. The demands of managing Trident were small. He had an excellent business manager in Jessica, who ran the headquarters in the Bahamas. His operations and logistics team in Abu Dhabi required almost no supervision. He would always be available for any missions assigned by Mike, but everything else was routine and easily managed by his subordinates. This was the perfect time to step back and release the reins to his younger aspirants.

Chapter 7

Bandar-e Jask, Iran

Colonel Shalmani and his team had been working tirelessly for the past four days. He and three other detachment commanders had received their orders at the Quds headquarters four days earlier in Tehran from Major General Suleimani himself. Colonel Shalmani was in awe of the great man. After the briefing, he was invited to tea in the commander's office.

An aide seated Colonel Shalmani at a side table next to the commander's desk. The Quds headquarters building had formerly housed the US embassy, and as the commander, Major General Suleimani could have claimed the lavish office of the former ambassador. Instead, his office was a small, nondescript twelve-by-twelve room on the first floor.

A tea service was placed on the table by a sergeant. Moments later, the great man entered. Colonel Shalmani jumped from his chair and stood at attention. The commander gestured for him to sit.

Dressed modestly in black slacks and shirt, the silver-haired two-star general was the epitome of understatement. Short in height at five-seven, he was lean and fit. He spoke softly and carried himself with a calmness that relaxed those around him.

The general poured Colonel Shalmani's tea and inquired about his wife and children. Suleimani used words sparingly.

He was a revered figure within the Quds Force. He avoided the spotlight and rarely drew attention to himself, so it was a rare honor to be invited to meet with him privately. Colonel Shalmani had always seen him as a role model and for years had imitated the great man's mannerisms and personality traits.

"What are your thoughts on the situation in Yemen?" asked the general.

"The Houthis are unreliable partners. They're blessed with a poorly trained opponent who lacks courage. I don't think either side has what it takes to achieve a total victory."

General Suleimani grinned, amused at his subordinate's words. "You don't believe with our support, the Houthis can drive out the Saudi invaders?"

"No, sir, I don't. The Houthis are bandits, not soldiers. They use our weapons to seize land and then they sell that same land back to the enemy. Eventually, they will be forced back into their ancestral lands in the mountains in the northwest of Yemen, and the remainder of southern and eastern Yemen will revert back to a Saudi puppet regime," Colonel Shalmani replied.

"The Houthis are serving their purpose. We're surrounding the Saudis. They're facing Shia opposition movements in the south from Yemen, the north from Iraq, and the east from Bahrain—and soon, hopefully from Oman and Qatar. It will take years, but eventually it will become too much, and the corrupt Saudi princes will abandon Arabia and retreat to their chateaus in Europe. The mission you're about to undertake in Oman is just another step in that grand strategy. Much is expected of you. You have demonstrated great skill in your past assignments, and in this next one, glory awaits you." With that, Suleimani stood to signal the end to the meeting.

While in Tehran, Colonel Shalmani was allowed only a few hours to meet with his wife and children, who lived in the capital. It had been months since he had last been at home. It was a Saturday, and fortunately his three children were not at school. The homecoming was quick. His wife, who was also his cousin, the daughter of his father's brother, was an obedient woman who never complained and managed well without him. He was thankful his parents had picked such a good wife for him. It was a very important thing, since he spent so little time at home.

Colonel Shalmani and the other leaders flew by military plane a thousand miles south to the Jask Naval Base on the Gulf of Oman and linked up with their respective teams. For the past four days, the naval base had been closed to all visitors, which had no doubt piqued the curiosity of the eleven thousand inhabitants of Jask. Colonel Shalmani and his team spent the next three days conducting dozens of day-and-night rehearsals of their respective missions. He was confident they were prepared for any contingency.

At ten in the evening, he boarded a Special Operations stealth boat and conducted a final equipment check. The thirty-two-foot gray vessel was a knockoff of the US Mark V. It was a sleek craft that resembled the shape of a cigarette boat. The boat had a crew of four Iranian Revolutionary Guard sailors and was capable of speeds of over fifty knots. The eight members of his team were seated in the high-impact shock-absorbing chairs that lined the rear open-air compartment. Tied down at the very back of the stern was a fifteen-foot rubber boat.

The four Special Operations boats left the docks at ten thirty. Each boat carried a team of nine Quds commandos and two sailors in the pilot's compartment, with two more sailors manning the heavy machine guns. Each boat had a different destination. The four objectives were all combined facilities consisting of power stations and desalinization plants. The respective Omani infrastructure targets were all located along the coast at Al-Ghubrah, Sohar, Barka I and Barka II. The combined output of the four plants accounted for more than eighty percent of Oman's water and power supply and represented one hundred percent of that used by the 2.4 million inhabitants of Muscat.

From Jask, it was almost a straight shot across the Gulf of Oman to Muscat. It was nearly midnight when Colonel Shalmani debarked the larger boat and loaded the team onto the fifteen-foot black rubber boat. The small outboard engine on the rubber boat had a noise dampener, allowing the boat to move almost soundlessly at a speed of eight knots through the misty dark waters.

The Al-Ghubrah power plant was located on the waterfront, half a mile east of the Chedi Hotel in the heart of Muscat. Even through the mist, the lights on the power plant smoke stacks were an easy beacon for Colonel Shalmani to guide on. The next two miles in the rubber boat were risky. The Omani Coast Guard would make quick work of them if they were ever discovered. The whisper engine strained to power the heavily laden boat; they would be outgunned and unable to outrun the sultan's Coast Guard. Compared to the Special Operations boat, it felt like a crawl.

Colonel Shalmani was in the far back of the raft, with his hand at the controls of the outboard. At the very front of the rubber boat, a commando lay in the prone position behind a 7.62mm PK machine gun he balanced on the bow. Three men on either side of the raft held 7.62mm AK-15 assault rifles pointed outward. One additional man sat on the right side of the boat, carrying an SVK sniper rifle. The men kneeled behind the thick rubber outer walls of the inflatable with their backpacks piled in the center.

The men were dressed in black combat uniforms and all wore night vision goggles mounted on their helmets. At their feet, each man had a large backpack filled with ammunition, explosives and breaching materials. The protection of the coastline and the power plant was the responsibility of the Royal Omani Police. Based on intelligence, Colonel Shalmani expected a force of between ten and fifteen police personnel defending the outer perimeter and the interior of the power plant. A greater threat was the response force from the Sultan's Special Forces Counter Terrorism Unit.

As soon as the boat beached, the men grabbed their rucksacks and filed out over the bow of the boat and onto the shore. The lead men had a hole cut in the chain-link fence surrounding the power station before Shalmani even exited the boat. The commandos moved silently in a column over the fifty meters to the concrete power plant building and then circled around the exterior of the building clockwise.

Shalmani moved to the head of the column and stopped the patrol when he identified the entrance to the guard shack on the side of the building with the main entrance. He signaled for the sniper to come forward. The sniper dropped to a prone position and crawled forward on his elbows until he had the guard shack within view and he was in a stable firing position.

Colonel Shalmani touched him on the leg, and seconds later the sniper dropped the lone guard with a suppressed shot to the head through the window of the shack. Immediately after the shot, the column of men bolted toward the power plant entrance. The door was locked, requiring a key card to enter. Shalmani gave the signal to emplace an explosive breach. He signaled for two of the men to ready a Bumblebee for action. Both removed RPO-A Shmell 93mm thermobaric rocket launchers that had been protruding from the tops of their rucksacks.

Unlike conventional explosives, thermobaric rounds didn't contain oxygen molecules. Instead, they used the oxygen from the surrounding air to generate intense high-temperature explosions, sometimes called fuel air explosives. The blast from a thermobaric round was much longer and more powerful than that of a conventional explosive. Thermobaric explosions removed all oxygen from a room, and the enhanced blasts created concussive forces that could knock out the walls in all but the strongest of structures.

Once the breaching charge exploded, the lead man pulled open the door and the team flowed into the plant. Using well-aimed single-shot fire, they cut down the unarmed civilians they found along their route to the first turbine room. After breaching the heavy steel entryway to the turbine room, the men began to meet resistance. The doorway that led into the turbine room was peppered with incoming gunfire, causing the team to stop their advance. Shalmani and his men all lay flat on the hallway floor, away from the door opening.

The first Bumblebee was launched from the hallway into the turbine room. The thermobaric explosion in the huge room was devastating. Flames shot back through the open door, and the shock wave leveled one of the exterior walls. The team jumped up from the floor and charged into the smoke-filled turbine room.

A two-man demo team instantly went to work emplacing shape charges on top of the turbine and the generator. The charges were connected by thirty feet of detonation cord. Once they lit the primary and backup time fuses, the team exited and continued the assault on the second turbine using the same techniques.

The last objective within the complex was the reverse-osmosis water plant. Well-placed explosives destroyed the pipeline connecting the RO plant to the city's reservoir and punctured the storage tanks.

The assault and destruction of the Al-Ghubra power station took only seventy-five minutes. Shalmani could hear the sirens as the police and fire departments began to respond. A column of first responders was held up at the locked outer gate.

The guard would not be of any help—the Quds sniper had made sure of that.

The response from the Counter-Terrorism team would take longer. Years of intelligence collection by Iranian spies recruited from the Shia population in Oman had confirmed that the Special Forces kept only one team on alert at any given time. The magnitude of four simultaneous attacks would simply overwhelm and paralyze the force. Shalmani expected the Omani Special Forces to defend instead of attack.

During the operation's planning, the Quds leaders had felt it was too dangerous to withdraw by sea. Royal Omani Navy patrol boats were always positioned near the power stations, and by the end of each mission, they would almost certainly be positioned offshore near the burning power plants. Instead, Colonel Shalmani and his team moved west, cutting through the perimeter fence line and then advancing into the palm-lined grass of Al-Ghubrah Park. The column of commandos walked westward parallel to the water until they reached a barren desert lot that separated the park from the Chedi Hotel complex.

The dirt road separating the barren lot and the Chedi Hotel was the extraction area where they were supposed to link up with their transportation. Shalmani was surprised to find the escape vehicles were not in position to extract them as planned. The two SUVs, driven by Iranian assets who lived in Oman, must have been held up by the police.

With the power to the city out, the only lights visible were the flames from the power station and the headlights and flashing blue and red lights of the emergency responders.

"We can't wait here much longer. The Army is going to arrive soon," one of his men said.

"We'll use vehicles from the hotel next door to get away. We're going to need a diversion. Get ready to fire the remaining Bumblebees."

Six of his men removed the rockets from their rucksacks.

"On my order, fire. Then we'll attack the valet station and take whatever SUVs we can find. If we break contact, link up at the safe house."

Colonel Shalmani guided his men forward and arrayed them in a line one hundred yards from the hotel. They were at the corner of the main building, where they could see the hotel front facing the main road with the lobby parking and a valet station. They also had a side view of the main hotel building that faced Al-Ghubrah Park.

"You three, aim for the hotel front, left." He pointed out a reference point for each soldier. Farhad and you two on the end, you aim for the side of the main building."

The men took a kneeling position, removed the launcher covers, disengaged the safeties and aimed. As soon as he saw everyone was ready, Shalmani gave the order to fire.

Unlike the power station, the hotel was not made of reinforced concrete. The rockets struck within seconds of each other, and the two-story structure was immediately engulfed by fire, followed by an enormous concussion. The blast blew the walls outward and collapsed the top floor into the first. The huge lobby tent was engulfed in flames, as were many of the surrounding palm trees. In seconds, the one-hundred-and-thirty-seven-room luxury hotel was reduced to nothing more than a burning heap.

At Colonel Shalmani's command, the men advanced in a line toward the valet station at a fast walk. Dozens of hotel patrons and workers were scattered on the ground outside the lobby area. The Quds commandos shot the civilians point-blank as they advanced.

Shalmani and four of his men commandeered a white Mercedes G63 SUV. The other four men stole a Nissan Patrol, the full sized SUV sold as Armada in the US. Without headlights, the men drove south in the dark along a rehearsed route, avoiding main roads and the police until they reached the safe house on the southern outskirts of Muscat.

Chapter 8

Muscat, Oman

An annoying beeping sound woke Pat from a deep sleep. It took a few seconds for him to recognize the source as the alarm on his uninterrupted power supply. Remembering that the UPS was good for only twenty minutes, he decided he'd better get a move on.

He went into the engine room and checked the breaker box. There was no power coming in from the external hookup. He pressed the ignition switch on the twenty-kilowatt generator, and the beeping sound stopped. He walked upstairs to the main salon and then went outside to the open stern. The marina was completely blacked out, and he was unable to see any lights from the Muscat skyline. He checked his cell phone and found there was no service.

Still barefoot and in his underwear, Pat went back into the salon through the gallery to the helm station and retrieved his iridium satphone. He threw on a bathrobe and went outside to get line of sight to a satellite. The first number he dialed was Susu's cell phone. The call didn't go through—there wasn't even a recording, just emptiness. Realizing power and cell service must be out citywide, he dialed Mike Guthrie's office at Langley next.

"Hello," Mike responded.

"This is Pat. Muscat just lost power and cell service. Are you tracking anything going on here from your end?"

"No, I'm kind of busy. Let me look into it and get back to you."

It took almost forty-five minutes before Mike returned his call.

"What's going on?" asked Pat.

"There's been an attack—a series of attacks. It looks like they went after the power plants."

"How bad is it?"

"We're still assessing. What little we have is from monitoring the police and military radio traffic."

"Don't you have satellite coverage?"

"No, all of our assets are committed. Hezbollah launched a rocket attack against Israel two hours ago. It's a bit chaotic at the moment."

"I'll go into town and see what I can find out."

"No sense getting on the road. If they haven't already declared martial law, they will. You'll just end up getting detained."

"I have a UAV on board my boat that has eight hours of air time and a range of fifty kilometers. Where should I send it?"

"Based on the traffic our station in Muscat is picking up, you should send it north to Barka and Al-Ghubra. I'll have someone send you a link so you can stream the video to our guys back here and to Walt's people. Do you have good internet communications?"

"Yeah, my satellite service is good. I have internet and can talk VoIP."

"Okay, gotta go."

After throwing on some clothes, Pat went to the tender that he was storing on the hydraulic ramp at the rear end of the stern. From underneath the tarp he removed a ten-foot-long waterproof bag that contained two components, a nine-foot wing and an eight-foot fuselage. He carried both components and a toolkit to the sundeck at the bow of the boat and connected the two pieces together.

The MartinUAV V-Bat weighed eighty-two pounds. Using one of the jerry cans from the engine room, he filled the UAV with a JP-8 mix. He stood the V-Bat upright with its nose pointing into the night sky and then retrieved a Kutta Tech ground control system from the engine room and carried it up to the flybridge. He connected the power and the antenna and then activated the system.

After running the diagnostics and verifying that the guidance, navigation, day camera and IR thermal cameras were all functioning, he used the map function and, using a mouse, selected waypoints for the aircraft to follow. He made sure to stay within the capabilities of the UAV. The advertised telemetry range for the V-Bat was fifty kilometers with the standard antenna, and the aircraft could be launched and recovered in a fifteen-by-fifteen-foot space. The sundeck in the bow of the boat fit the bill perfectly as a launch and recovery platform.

He set a preprogramed route to follow the waypoints at an altitude of five thousand feet and a speed of thirty knots. The control station consisted of two connected rugged laptop computers. One computer controlled and displayed the aircraft's flight data and location, while the second computer controlled the two cameras that were located at the base of the fuselage on a gimbal and displayed the imagery. After almost an hour of preparation, Pat started the UAV engines and launched the VTOL (vertical take off and landing) aircraft.

The V-Bat looked like any other UAV of its size, except that at the base of the fuselage, it had a large rotor protected by a sturdy duct. Looking down from the table on the flybridge, Pat could see the narrow fuselage, the two wings jutting out at a ninety-degree angle and the big basket at the base of the aircraft, which gave it the look of a bowling pin with wings. Beneath the basket protecting the propeller were short legs used for launching and landing.

The aircraft was loud, sounding like a gas lawn mower on full throttle as it ascended vertically into the night sky. At five hundred feet, the computer controls transitioned the aircraft from a rotary wing hover into airplane mode, and it moved out of sight as it began its journey to survey the coastline.

The noise of the launch drew some attention from his follow boaters. Only a few of the boats in the marina were occupied; it was easy to see which ones, because they were illuminated either by onboard generators or flashlights and lanterns.

Pat dressed and made himself some coffee, then returned to his control station on the flybridge table with a third laptop computer. This one was his personal PC and not ruggedized. After checking his email to get the link, he connected his computer to the imagery laptop using an HDMI cable and began to stream the video to Langley and to Walt's people at the embassy in Muscat.

It was dark, so he set the camera selection to IR. He played with different settings. When the thermal camera was at low magnification at an altitude of five thousand feet, he could detect people, homes and cars. When he switched the setting to high magnification, the thermal optics could count the fingers on a person's hand. He switched to the day camera, but all that confirmed was that the city was completely blacked out. He found military and police checkpoints set up across the city, with heavy armored combat vehicles blocking most major intersections. The city was clearly in a high state of alarm.

The first waypoint was the Al-Ghubrah power and desalinization station. At thirty knots, it took less than twenty minutes to reach Al-Ghubrah, where he triggered the loiter selection using the touchpad. The aircraft began to do tight circles around the power station while maintaining an altitude of five thousand feet.

He began to receive instant messages from the Langley analysts on his personal laptop. Change from thermal to day camera. Go to high magnification. Go to low magnification. Orient on the desalinization water storage tanks. From the air, the damage to the power station didn't look very severe. The only telltale sign was a small amount of debris and flooding near the desalinization tanks.

He picked up a large fire northwest of the power station, half a mile further up the coastline, so he turned off the loiter option and let the aircraft continue further along its preprogrammed course until it was directly over the fire. He then reengaged the loiter option and began to search the area with the small joystick that controlled the thermal optics.

It took a few minutes before Pat was able to determine that it was the Chedi Hotel he was looking at. Unlike the power station and the desalinization plant, the devastation to the hotel was absolute. The main building was completely consumed by fire, and from the air he could see dozens of bodies splayed around the structure. Fire trucks and police were on the scene. The firefighting efforts were ineffective; the main building and many of the smaller outbuildings were completely consumed by flames.

Pat was furious at himself for not having Susu's satphone number. He wasn't even sure if she had a satphone. He racked his brain trying to remember if she had told him where she was going to be last night, but he couldn't remember.

After surveying the scene for thirty minutes, the analysts at Langley requested that Pat move the UAV to the Barka facility, which was another fifteen miles from the Chedi and near the limit of the V-Bat's range.

The scene at Barka was similar to Al-Ghubrah. The Barka facility consisted of two power stations (Barka I and Barka II) and a desalinization plant. From the air, he could find some structural damage to the turbine buildings, but as in the previous case, most of the damage was contained inside the buildings. Pat was having difficulty concentrating. The anxiety of not knowing Susu's status was starting to eat at him.

After thirty minutes of surveying the Barka complex, he instructed the autopilot to return the aircraft to the launch location. He called Mike from his satphone.

"The sun is going to be up soon. All the roads are blocked. I'm going to anchor my boat off the coast of the Chedi and then go in with my tender and have a closer look. I might need some backup from the US embassy to vouch for me. The security folks won't be happy to see me."

"Why the Chedi?" replied Mike.

"It's been completely destroyed, it looks like a major bombing. I want to find out what happened and how many people got hurt."

"Does it look like a lot of casualties?"

"From the UAV, I couldn't tell, but I didn't see any major collection areas of people who escaped the fire, only small pockets of guests or employees."

"How many people were staying at the hotel?"

"It was full. I'd guess at least two hundred, not including staff. Quite a few Americans. I'm worried about Susu."

"Walt has a satphone. I'll have him contact you. Tell any of the officials who challenge you that you're from the embassy, office of diplomatic security. Walt will back you up. He'll get the ambassador to vouch for you if needed."

"How goes the war between Lebanon and Israel?"

"Don't expect much help in Oman. All eyes are on Tel Aviv, Southern Beirut, Saudi and Tehran. This is turning very ugly."

"At least we know who attacked Israel," Pat said.

"ISIS has claimed credit for the attack in Oman."

"Do you believe that?"

"I don't know. The trouble is there are just as many parties that want chaos and civil war in Oman as those who don't. It could be ISIS, AQAP or even Houthis, but we're leaning more towards Iran."

"Oman is neutral. They're a major trading partner to Iran. What's the motivation?"

"Oman and Lebanon are pawns in the war between Iran and Saudi. Another civil war on the Arabian Peninsula is a good thing from the Iranians' viewpoint."

"I'm having trouble understanding that, but I have more practical things to worry about. I have to run. I'll let you know what I find out."

"I hope Susu is safe."

"You and me both."

After retrieving and storing the V-Bat, Pat cast off the connections and ropes binding the *Sam Houston*. The sun was rising when he eased the boat from its slip and guided it out of the marina and into the deeper waters of the Gulf of Oman. Before casting off, he made sure the American flag was prominently displayed above the flybridge. He anticipated the Omani Navy would be in a shoot-first-and-ask-questions-later mood and didn't want to encourage them.

He kept the boat a mile from the shore as he traveled west along the shoreline. It was only thirteen miles to the Chedi, and he didn't expect the trip to take long. As he came within range, the first damage he saw in the early-morning light was to the Al-Ghubrah power plant. With his binoculars, he could see charring on the ground level. Doors were blown out and one wall had been leveled. The desalinization tanks were ruptured, and water pooled everywhere.

As Pat studied the damaged building from the flybridge, an Omani police patrol boat intersected him and signaled him to heave to. Pat cut the engines, and two members of the forty-five-foot patrol boat boarded the *Sam Houston* while a machine gunner menacingly trained his weapon on Pat. The boarding party entered the boat from the starboard side rail.

"Show me your ID," a nervous captain ordered in English.

Pat gave the captain a red US diplomatic passport.

"My name is Pat Walsh. I'm assigned to the US embassy, and I have been requested by the ambassador to use my personal boat to visit the Chedi and assess the loss of American lives."

"I'm afraid you have to turn back. No vessels can enter into this area."

"The US is not being given any information from the Omani government. I insist you allow me to pass, so that I can do my job and gain an understanding of the loss of American lives last night. I have a satellite phone. If you want, I can patch you through to my direct supervisor."

"You must turn back. This area is off-limits."

"It may be off-limits to some, but I represent the US government. Many of the guests in that hotel were American, and because of your security, many are now dead. My job now is to survey the consequences of your failure and submit a report. I suggest you make some calls on that radio of yours, because I'm not going anywhere," Pat said forcefully, leaving no doubt that he was not going to take no for an answer.

The captain retreated to his own craft, and the two boats remained tied to each other for forty-five minutes while the captain sorted through the Omani military confusion and bureaucracy. Finally, the captain reboarded the *Sam Houston*.

"You may proceed. Check in with Colonel Al-Busaidi when you get to shore," he said as he handed Pat back his passport.

Pat anchored one thousand yards directly offshore from the hotel. He carefully avoided the area roped off for swimming to avoid fouling the propeller on the outboard motor of his eleven-foot tender. The temperature was sixty-five degrees. It was a cool morning, and the inversion layer created by the weather kept the smoke low to the ground. The final approach to the beach was through near darkness because of a heavy pall of dark gray smoke that hung like a thick blanket over the area.

After beaching the tender, Pat tossed the small anchor onto the beach and jumped into the knee-high surf to make his way to the hotel. Wearing a pair of gray Patagonia pants and a black Underarmour T-shirt with a Nikon D5200 strapped around his neck, he walked through the dense smoke until he reached the remains of the main building.

Although several of the outer buildings were still in flames, the main building had already completely burned itself out. As he traversed the main building, where most of the guest rooms were located, it was readily apparent that few people had escaped. The two-story building had collapsed in on itself. Pat continued to survey the building as he circled around it clockwise until he found the front. In the lobby area, for the first time, he found signs of battle. Empty brass bullet cartridges were scattered around the driveway and parking area in what had previously been the hotel entrance.

Pat inspected one of the 7.62x39mm cartridges. He could tell they were Russian spec and not NATO 7.62x51mm because they were shorter. He took several samples to allow the technicians to identify the factory that had manufactured the rounds. As he was collecting the ammunition, an officer wearing the green camouflage and tan beret of the Sultan's Special Forces challenged him.

"Who are you?" the major barked in English.

"I'm looking for Colonel Al-Busaidi. He's expecting me. Take me to him," Pat barked back.

Colonel Al-Busaidi was a tall, fit man. He had a well-trimmed black beard, and he was surrounded by a circle of junior officers and civilians in local dress, white kandora or dishdasha and red-and-white patterned headscarves called kaffiyeh, when the major escorted Pat to him.

"*Salaam alaikum,*" the colonel said upon seeing him.

"*Wa alaikum salaam,*" Pat replied as the two men shook hands.

"You're with the United States government?"

"Yes, I'm here to gather information for our embassy," replied Pat.

"You're CIA?"

"No, I'm with the Diplomatic Security Service." Pat removed the iridium satphone from his cargo pocket. "Would you like to speak with my superiors in the US?" he asked.

"Not necessary. What would you like to know?"

"The basics. Who did this and where are they now?"

"We believe this was an attack by the Iranians. Our coastal radar tracked four small vessels last night advancing against our coastline at around midnight. Four power stations and desalinization plants were attacked within one hour of each other. Barka I and Barka II further up the coast to the north, Al-Ghubrah next to us, and Sohar to our south. Following the attack in Al-Ghubrah, the same team came to this hotel and attacked it with RPGs. The launcher tubes are over there." The colonel pointed to the edge of the hotel grounds.

"The RPGs were thermobaric. They created a huge fire which has killed many of the hotel guests. It's going to take days to fully recover the bodies and much longer to identify them. The registrations were all electronic, and because of the damage and lack of power, we don't have a list of the guests. At this time, we estimate the casualty numbers to be over one hundred."

"How long before power is restored?" Pat asked.

"We don't know."

"Any idea on the current location of the Iranian commandos?" asked Pat.

"None."

"Will you accept US assistance in tracking them down?"

The fatigue and desperation on the colonel's face required no response. He nodded.

"Do you have a satphone?"

"No."

"Do you have a generator?"

"No."

"Where's your headquarters?"

"It's going to be here, for a while anyway."

"Sir, I have a portable Honda 1.5-kilowatt generator and an extra satphone in my boat. I'll go back and get you those items. We need to stay in contact. The US has assets that might help you in searching for these Iranians. The Iranians only have two options after an attack like this. They're either going to escape, which means right now they're heading toward the Yemeni border, or they're going to remain in Muscat and hit additional targets. You need to seal the border as much as possible."

"The order to seal the border has already been given. You think they'll hit us again tonight?"

"They won't attack in the daylight, and there's no sense in waiting until you get the lights turned back on. So, yeah, if they aren't already on the run, they'll probably take advantage of the situation and attack again," Pat replied.

He returned to the yacht and supplied the colonel with the generator and the satphone. He photographed what was left of the hotel and inspected and then took photos of the Bumblebee thermobaric rocket launcher tubes. From the markings, he could tell they were made in Russia, which pointed toward the Iranians. Recovery efforts were underway.

Before he left, he went to the area next to the swimming pool, where the bodies were being lined up. There were forty-two bodies, most too badly burned to identify. He only saw two that could possibly have been a female of Susu's size, but he discounted them upon closer inspection.

Although he didn't have any proof, he had a sick feeling that she was among the casualties. Susu was always able to contact him when she wanted to, and she would know he was worried about her. He had a satphone, and his boat had satellite Wi-Fi, which gave him internet VoIP, instant messaging and email. Getting ahold of him wouldn't be that hard.

Something was tragically wrong. He decided to ask Walt to check with the Chinese government just to be sure.

Chapter 9

Muscat, Oman

When Pat returned to his slip in Al-Bustan Marina, he noticed Walt Berg standing on the walkway. He backed the *Sam Houston* in using the joystick in the stern control station. Walt helped Pat tie the boat down and met Pat in the salon afterward.

"Do you want a drink?" asked Pat.

"No, I need to stay sharp. It's going to be another late night."

"Did you get any news on Susu?"

"Sorry, no. The identification of the bodies is going slow."

"We have the Fifth Fleet a few miles away in Bahrain. We should send some mortuary assets. You should have seen the hotel. The Omanis don't have clue how to handle the situation. They're leaving the bodies out in the sun. It's terrible," Pat said.

"Assets are on the way. Believe it or not, there's a lot being done."

"I'm sure there is. The man in charge of the attack site was Colonel Al-Busaidi. He seemed like a heavy hitter. Who is he?" Pat asked.

"He commands the Cobras. They're the counterterrorist squadron within the Sultan's Special Forces," Walt replied.

"His English was perfect, and he seemed switched on, very professional. I offered US support to help him track and kill the Iranian teams, and he accepted," Pat said.

"This is not a good time for you to go rogue."

"I don't intend to. That's why I called you to meet me. We need to plan, and then we need to work the phones to get support assets."

"What kind of assets are you talking about?" Walt asked.

"The cell phone service is down. We have four Iranian teams, A-team sized at maybe ten to twelve operators each. They need to coordinate with each other, and they need to communicate back to Tehran for reporting and extraction. If they can't use GSM, they'll need to communicate either UHF/VHF or satellite. We should get some SIGINT assets over Muscat to detect them and locate them," Pat said.

"That makes sense. What did you have in mind?"

"Guard Rail, Rivet Joint, Global Hawk, whatever is available. It's going to be dark in a couple of hours, and I think the bad guys are either going to use the night to make a run to the Yemen border or they're going to hit more targets. Who knows, maybe even do both," Pat said.

"What targets do you think they'll hit next?"

"I don't know. After the power, water and communications, the next best high-value targets should be either economic or political," Pat said.

"Oil and gas is all there is as far as the economy goes."

"Agreed. By now, I imagine all the political targets are protected and in hiding. Hopefully that's especially true for the new sultan, if they attack, it'll be the oil and gas facilities," Pat said.

"Definitely, although the oil fields are huge. They're too spread out to defend," Walt said.

"Knocking out an oil well hardly seems worthwhile. I'd go for the pipelines, refineries and storage facilities. Those would create the most havoc," Pat said.

"Let me talk to my Department of Defense counterparts and submit some support requests."

"You'll have to coordinate with the Omani government. Who's in charge anyway?" Pat said.

"Sultan Asaad accepted the throne today in a small rushed ceremony. About the only people who know that in Oman are the people inside Al-Bustan Palace."

"I'm sure the military bases have their own generators. Knocking out the power stations shouldn't hurt defense," Pat said.

"The bigger problem is potable water. The reservoir that supports Muscat holds only a seven-day supply of water. Knocking out the desalinization stations that fed the reservoir means that in a week, the population is going to run out of water," Wall said with dread in his voice.

"I'm sure they'll ration it and start trucking it in from UAE and Saudi."

"It's going to take a couple of days to get a new water delivery system going, and it won't be easy to replace pipelines with trucks. Rationing is going to cause serious hardship; the population is not going to have a lot of confidence in the new sultan. If the Omanis don't solve this crisis soon, Sultan Asaad is going to have a hard time gaining the support of the Omani people," Walt said.

"When you request the intel support from DoD, you should also ask for some shooters. We need Blackhawks, Apaches and at least four teams of operators. We can base them out of the airport, and once the intel birds find the bad guys, all you'll have to do is vector in the assaulters," Pat said.

Walt walked through the triple door separating the salon from the stern deck. Pat could see him through the window making phone calls on a satphone. He walked over to the bar and filled a whiskey tumbler with two inches of Macallan 18. He found his laptop on the galley table, opened it up and made a Skype call to Roger McDonald in Abu Dhabi.

"Roger, it's time to get busy."

"What do you need?"

"Do we have an aircraft available?"

"Yes, both are in Darfur."

"Recall whichever crew is the most rested. I need them and the ops guys ready to fly on thirty minutes' notice. Flight plan is to Oman. Email me a list of possible landing strips along the coast, from Muscat to the Yemeni border. Borrow two of the Flyer vehicles from the Mali order and load them up. You'll need supplies for two to three days. Four teams of Iranian Special Forces took out the Omani power grid last night. If you get a call, it'll be because the Omani and US forces are already committed."

"We're the reinforcements?"

"It's all last-minute. The Omanis are headless chickens and the JSOTF from Bahrain is just now being notified. I'm just trying to build some backup capability in case one of the Iranian teams slips away into the desert. I want to be able to hunt them down."

"If we're on a thirty-minute string, it will take us another thirty to forty minutes to get to Muscat, and probably about ninety minutes total to get to the border of Yemen. You're going to need some good lead time if you're going to use us. Wouldn't it be better to pre-position us in Muscat Airport?"

"The airport is closed to everything except military aircraft. The airport is degraded because of the power outage. The Omanis are in the third stage of polio. No power, no water, no government to speak of. I can't bring you in until it's time to go hot."

"When you do call, make sure somebody lets the Omani Air Force know we're the good guys."

"Of course."

After the call with Roger, Pat fell lengthwise onto the salon couch and pressed the remote control to raise the big-screen TV from inside the cabinet. He worked through the satellite news channels until he settled on BBC, which always seemed to have the best international coverage. He was sipping his scotch, engrossed in the story of President Saleh's execution at the hands of the Houthis in Sana'a, Yemen, when Walt returned to the salon.

"Is there anything else that could make this day any worse?" asked Pat.

"That happened last night. You just finding out now?"

"Yeah, I guess I'm still catching up on events. Iran attacks Oman. Lebanon attacks Israel. The head of the Yemeni rebels who was going to agree to peace with the Saudis has been whacked by the Houthis, extending the war for God knows much longer. What else could go wrong in this magical, peaceful place we call the Middle East?"

"That about covers it."

"Were you able to get some assets from DoD?"

"It's not one hundred percent final, but it looks that way."

"Is there an operations center somewhere that will have the American and Omani military leadership running this Iranian hunt?"

"There's an American Air Force squadron that operates out of Muscat Airport. They have an air operations center that will be coordinating with the CAOC in Al-Udeid in Qatar for all air assets. The Sultan's Special Forces will have a cell in the AOC for intelligence reasons. The Bahrain JSOTF is planning on deploying two SEAL teams to support the SSF. The SEALs will arrive in two MH-60s with two AH-64s for support."

"That's pretty lean. Seriously, is that all Uncle Sam could spare?"

"Everything is coming apart right now in the region, as you've already mentioned. The SOF forces in Bahrain have high-priority contingency missions to evacuate US personnel in Lebanon and in other places, including possibly Oman."

"What about the intel assets?"

"That's more of a good news story. We'll have complete coverage of the entire coastline and the Yemeni border. Plus, the Omani military is deploying forces to secure critical infrastructure, including oil and gas facilities."

"I'll bet that team that hit the Chedi isn't more than thirty minutes from here right now. I sure hope they decide to use a radio."

"I asked the embassy to make an official inquiry to the Chinese embassy regarding Susu. The Chinese haven't responded yet."

"The Chinese won't respond, knowing them. If she was alive, she would've contacted me by now."

"You're handling it pretty well."

"It helps to have something to do. Plus, she was a colonel in the army. She's not the first soldier I've ever known to die in the line of duty."

"I thought she was a little more than that."

"She was, but it's best to compartmentalize."

"I remember when something like this happened before, if you don't mind me saying, you went a little crazy."

"That was different. She wasn't a combatant. In this situation, the Iranians were doing their job, Susu was doing her job, and hopefully, once those spy planes go to work, I'll get a chance to do my job. Nothing personal about it, just everybody doing their duty."

Walt met Pat's eyes as he was speaking. What he saw must have disturbed him, because he quickly looked away.

"Is there someone in the AOC that I can communicate with, or do I need to go there myself?"

"That's where I'm going now. I'll keep you updated."

"In addition to the SSF and the JSOTF guys, my team is on alert in Abu Dhabi. They can get to Muscat in less than an hour from notification. Just in case."

"They'll be the third option."

"That's fine, but if I call you, please make sure they get airspace clearance. I don't want a jumpy Omani fighter pilot shooting them out of the sky."

"Will do."

Chapter 10

Muscat, Oman

Colonel Shalmani sat on the thick Persian carpet on the living room floor. Seated on cushions along the surrounding walls were his eight men. The family who owned the safe house had remained on the second floor of the villa since they had arrived in the early-morning hours.

The home was in the Darsalt neighborhood of Muscat, roughly ten miles east along the coast from the Chedi Hotel, where they had attacked only hours previously. It was a modest two-story villa in a mostly working-class neighborhood across from an Indian school and down the street from a Lulu supermarket.

After all the men had slept, washed, prayed and eaten, Colonel Shalmani had gathered them together in the living room to brief them on the next mission.

"The refinery is fifteen hundred meters from our location, due west. The terrain is very difficult. We need to cross a steep hill with a narrow trail that will lead us right on top of the refinery gate. Once we breach the outer security fence, the refinery is broken up into quadrants. Each two-man team will have sixty minutes to set their charges and get back to the breach point in the fence. I will detonate the explosives exactly at sixty minutes, so don't be late."

It was a simple plan that had been rehearsed extensively in Iran. The purpose of the briefing was just to refresh their memories. Men from the Iranian embassy had been stockpiling explosives shipped in diplomatic pouches for many months. The family who occupied the home were Omani citizens, but members of a Shia resistance group.

All four teams had been instructed to maintain radio silence until they were at the extraction points. Colonel Shalmani had no information on the status of the other teams. He assumed they had been successful because of the lack of electricity and the lockdown of the city. Until he returned to Tehran, he would likely not know how things went.

At one in the morning, the men filed out of the home. Each was burdened with fifteen two-pound RDX explosive charges connected to a receiver inside his rucksack. The men carried AK-15s with PEQ IR lasers for aiming, and all wore night vision goggles mounted on their helmets.

The hill was steep, and the trail was narrow and poorly marked. While climbing to the top, several of the men slipped and fell, cutting themselves on the sharp rocks. When the men reached the top, Colonel Shalmani had them pause for water and rest. Before descending, he positioned a sniper at the edge of the hill overlooking the Mina al Fahal refinery complex, where he could cover their movement with his SVK sniper rifle.

The descent down the hill was even more treacherous than the climb up. Several of the men lost their footing and slid down the steep slope, incurring more cuts and bruises. Once they reached the bottom of the hill, the fence was easily breached with a pair of wire cutters.

"Set your watches, and be back here no later than one hour," the colonel whispered.

The four teams moved out at a jog. Colonel Shalmani and his teammate worked one of the two quadrants adjacent to the breach point, so they moved with less haste. Inside the area were six large oil tanks and a series of thick pipes that moved the fuel into and out of the refinery facility. Colonel Shalmani and his teammate split up and began attaching their explosive charges and activating the receivers.

The refinery complex was close to a square mile. It had a road going around it and several other roads that crisscrossed the complex. Because of the blackout, the refinery was shut down and there were no lights. Twice Colonel Shalmani had to stop and find cover because a police patrol vehicle passed by. It was a cool night, but by the time Colonel Shalmani returned to the cut in the fence line, his clothing was soaked through with sweat.

At the sixty-minute mark, three of the teams, including his own, were at the breach point. He decided to wait five more minutes. He had the Shrike Exploder sitting on his rucksack. The detonator was a dark green six-inch plastic cube that weighed slightly more than a pound. The device had four independent firing circuits. Each quadrant was on a separate firing frequency.

He turned on and tested the system and then selected all four frequencies to fire simultaneously. As he was readying the device, he heard his last two soldiers climb through the fence line. He told his men to get down and everyone hit the dirt and covered their ears. He pressed the rubber prime and firing buttons at the same time with the index fingers of both hands. The sky erupted in a fiery yellow-and-orange explosion, and seconds later a deafening noise pounded his eardrums.

A blast of hot air swept over the men. The Iranian commandos jumped to their feet and scrambled up the steep hill. With lighter, nearly empty rucksacks and the adrenaline rush from the blast, the trip up the hill took less than five minutes. Joined by the sniper, the men retreated down the other side of the hill and returned to the safe house.

The explosion woke the neighborhood, and the team's movement down the narrow unlit street to the safe house did not go unnoticed. Instead of entering the house, the men loaded up in the two white Toyota Land Cruiser SUVs parked behind the gate. The vehicles had been left inside the villa walls weeks earlier by the Iranian embassy personnel.

The plan was to use the disruption from the refinery to escape for the Yemeni border. Both vehicles had been topped off with fuel and loaded with extra five-gallon jerry cans for the six-hundred-mile trip.

The trip to the Yemeni border would take nine hours. If movement was only restricted to the night, it would require two days' travel. The first leg was to Haima, located in the center of Oman; the second leg would take them across the border into Saudi and then Yemen.

Despite the five-hundred-foot hill between the house and the refinery, Colonel Shalmani could see a bright glow in the night sky from the enormous uncontained fires sweeping through the refinery and the nearby storage tanks. Occasionally, the air was punctuated by secondary explosions as fuel tanks became engulfed in the spreading conflagration.

A gentle breeze blew in from the ocean. His nose was beginning to itch and his eyes sting from the noxious fumes created by the burning fuel and chemicals. Realizing he had waited long enough, he signaled the drivers to exit through the villa gate and join the convoy of other neighborhood residents fleeing from the growing toxic cloud emanating from the refinery.

The hazardous fumes produced a flood of traffic, creating a traffic jam fleeing where the many small neighborhood roads converged with the major arteries. Soldiers manning the road blocks were forced to open the intersections to the escaping civilians. Fire and police vehicles added to the congestion on the roads. Armed soldiers manning roadblocks waved Colonel

Shalmani's SUV through all four of the main intersections on his way to the Muscat Expressway and Highway 31, which would lead him to Haima.

Chapter 11

The noise from the refinery explosion woke Pat. Years in the military had made him a light sleeper who could instantly be alerted by a radio call. Using the yacht's Wi-Fi, he sent an instant message to Walt.

"Just heard an explosion, what's going on?" he typed.

"Refinery in Sohar and LNG storage facility in Suhr have been hit. UAV coverage from Doha has eyes on both teams. Assault teams are about to launch from here to intercept," Walt responded.

"That's great. The explosion I just heard is a lot closer than either of those locations," Pat replied.

"We vectored the UAVs to the first two incidents. We have one more UAV over Muscat, but we don't have any targets. There are reports of a fourth attack just north of Muscat. We have the UAV overhead looking for targets, and we have an SSF unit moving on the ground to intercept if we find something."

"It sounds like you have things under control."

"We just received positive ID on the third team from the intel cell in the CAOC. SSF is moving to intercept."

"That still leaves the fourth team that just woke me up as location unknown."

"We're out of assets."

"I'm going to move my team south to the border. Once you're done with the fights around Muscat, you should focus south. The last team has to be on the road, running for the border."

"Okay. Bring your guys in, let me know when and where. I'll get them cleared. We still have the SIGINT assets. If anybody talks, we'll find them."

Pat sat on the long couch at the stern of the *Sam Houston* and looked out at the unlit darkness of Muscat. He dialed McDonald on his satphone.

"What's the closest airstrip to the Yemeni border you can use?"

"We found a strip by Al-Mazyunah."

"Go there now. Send me the long-lat, I'll get the air clearance. Three teams are being engaged by the SEALs and the Sultan's Special Forces. The fourth got away and should be running for the border."

"What do you want us to do?"

"Once you disembark, get to the nearest highway and wait. The US has a lot of intel assets trying to find them. Once they do, your job will be to stop them. Ideally we'll be able to give you enough lead time to set up an ambush."

"It's going to take us ninety minutes to get there."

"The attack happened less than ten minutes ago, and it's a nine-hour drive to the border, so you have plenty of time. I'm going to drive down to Al-Mazyunah now. Before you leave make sure you send me a satphone number I can reach you at."

"Okay, boss, moving now."

"Roger out."

Pat filled a large gym bag with clothes and gear and loaded it into his rented Ford Explorer, along with two cases of bottled water and three five-gallon gas cans he borrowed from the engine room, before locking up the *Sam Houston*. He had to leave the generator running because there was no external power and he didn't want the food in his refrigerator to spoil. There was enough fuel on board to run the generator for many months, but it wasn't something he wanted to try.

The border between Yemen and Oman was a straight line one hundred and fifty miles long, well secured with a strong fence and barbed wire. There were three crossing sites: one near the coast, one near the Saudi border and one in the center at Al-Mazyunah. The border between Oman and Yemen had been closed since May of 2016 for security reasons, but the rough terrain along the coast was a popular smuggling route, and for all intents and purposes, the border had remained partially open. Since the attacks the previous night, the Omani military had reinforced the border crossings with armored vehicles and increased patrols.

Pat was stopped twice at military checkpoints before reaching the highway. Both times he had to call Walt, who would hand the satphone over to an SSF officer in the AOC, who then ordered the soldiers manning the road blocks to let him pass. Once he was on Highway 31, he had almost four hundred miles before his next turn, which gave him plenty of time to think. He had the escaping Iranians ahead of him, most likely traveling on the same highway with a head start of at least an hour. His team was going to be in Al-Mazyunah shortly.

An idea came to him, and he called Mike Guthrie.

"How goes the chaos management?"

"I haven't been getting much sleep, and tonight looks like another all-nighter. What do you need?" Mike replied testily.

"I'm assuming Walt is keeping you up to date on what's happening here?"

"Yeah. Three of the Iranian teams have been destroyed. No prisoners, they all fought to the end. The two largest refineries in Oman were destroyed. The only natural gas storage facility and the only natural gas pipeline were destroyed. Oh yeah, and the largest oil pipeline that moved product from the oil fields to the coast for shipment was also blown up."

"What's the impact of all that?"

"Combined with the destruction of the power plants and desalinization plants, our analysts are saying the northern half of Oman has been returned to the seventh century. It's going to take years to recover, and during that recovery period, they're going have very few oil revenues. Qaboos kept the population under control with the carrot and the stick. Without any carrots, which is the ability to pay the citizens off with benefits, Sultan Asaad is going to be reduced to maintaining control by force. Using only the stick leads to either tyranny or revolution. It's a very bleak situation."

"Will Oman go back to Dhofar rebellion days?" asked Pat.

"Possibly. Very few of the tribes have any loyalty to Sultan Asaad, and if he doesn't keep the people in the style of living they've grown accustomed to, it makes sense they would want to get rid of him."

"I imagine that's going to make your job more difficult."

"The region is on fire. Most of our energy is focused on Israel and Lebanon at the moment."

"That's why I'm calling. We need to find this last Iranian team, and we don't have the assets we need. Can I get David Forrest and his guys involved? If the intel cell in the CAOC ported the sensor feeds to Dave, he could bring some serious computing power that might help us find these guys."

"The problem is the security issue."

"He has the highest clearances possible from UK. We have a SCIF at Paphos complete with a SIPRNET connection. It's a NATO intel exchange."

"You don't think you'll find this last team without him?"

"No, I don't. They're definitely exfilling to Yemen. The Oman border is pretty well covered, but the more I think about it, it makes more sense for the Iranians to jump the Oman-Saudi fence and then go into Yemen through Saudi."

"I don't have the authority to change security rules. If I go to the director, I'm afraid he'll decline the request. We've got three out of four teams; the priority now is security in Oman. An Iranian team running away from Oman isn't much of a security threat."

"This team we're after are the ones who hit the Chedi."

"How do you know that?"

"Proximity. They hit the Mina al Fahal refinery early this morning, which is the closest night-two objective to the Chedi Hotel. The teams would have hit their respective night-one objectives, gone to the closest safe house and then hit the closest night-two objectives. That's the only sensible way to do it. There's no way it would have been another team."

"I get that you want payback because of your girlfriend. You have my sympathy, believe me, but that won't sway the director."

"What about the Americans killed in the Chedi? The director isn't going to want to let their killers get away. How many did we lose, anyway?"

"Based on missing persons reports and data on who was staying at the Chedi, we believe the total is sixty-one. Forensic identifications are going to take months."

"Hunting down the Chedi massacre killers seems like a priority the director will have."

"Yeah, you might be right. I'll check and get back to you ASAP."

The next call Pat made was to David Forrest in Paphos, Cyprus. It was almost three in the morning when Pat woke the professor. After a lengthy explanation about the Iranians and the sensor feeds that were hopefully going to come from Doha, David was satisfied that he had enough of a target profile to work with.

Pat was able to fill up on fuel at a service station in Haima. The power grid in the southern half of Oman was thankfully still operating. Central Oman was open, desolate desert, flat and barren. Haima was the largest population center with ten thousand people widely dispersed, an oil town with few luxuries. Pat was pleased to find a Shell station with a restroom and a restaurant.

By the time he finished his breakfast, he was recharged. His team was on the ground. Clearwater was fully engaged in searching for the Chedi killers. The loss of Susu was going to take a while to process. The task of planning and executing an operation was a welcome distraction. Driving in central Oman was about the closest thing to sensory deprivation possible. The only break from the flat brown landscape was the narrow highway. He tried hard to stay alert, because of sand drifts. Winds were constantly blowing sand onto the highway and it was important to stay alert because running into a sand dune on a highway could be fatal.

Pat was grateful to leave the drab, flat brownness of central Oman and enter the southern Dhofar region, with its beautiful rocky outcroppings and occasional greenery. He followed the Explorer's navigation system to the coordinates Roger McDonald had given him and left the highway, taking an exit that led him onto a treacherous path. The narrow trail was rocky, and spires of copper-colored rocks jutted out all around. If he slipped off the road, his vehicle risked being impaled by the landscape. He gained elevation and then several miles later descended into a valley that contained a dirt airstrip.

He was surprised to find not only his team with the two Flyer tactical vehicles parked, but the Hercules C-130J that had flown them in. He had been driving for nine hours with only two fuel breaks, and he was grateful to finally reach his destination.

He was warmly greeted by the team. Migos met him as he was getting out of the truck.

"Why is the plane still here?" Pat asked.

"It's a maintenance issue. They had a warning light and they needed to check it out."

The two men joined McDonald, Burnia and Jankowski, who were all sitting in field chairs around a fire. Propped up by stones above the fire was a round barbeque grill grate.

"That smells really good. My last meal was some really sketchy falafel at a gas station."

Burnia threw a pack of round Arabic bread to Pat. He removed one of the pieces and used it like an oven mitt to smother a chicken breast and remove it from the hot grill. Pat ate while he listened to the friendly banter between Migos and Burnia.

"You have no game. I take you to the best pool party with the hottest girls in Abu Dhabi and you act you like the head of the Pokémon club at a junior high dance."

"Migos, those were not the hottest girls in Abu Dhabi. That one you left with looked like a troll."

"You're making excuses to cover your inadequacies."

"Because I didn't hit on Shrek's sister? Are you serious?"

Pat finished his chicken and changed the topic.

"It might be to our advantage that we still have the C-130," Pat said.

"Why is that?" asked Roger McDonald.

"When I propositioned you down here near the border, I thought that was where the Iranians were heading. But after thinking about it for most of the trip, I think the Iranians will cross into Saudi and enter Yemen that way."

"The western half of the Saudi-Yemen border is controlled by the Houthis. If they crossed into Yemen from Oman or from the eastern half, they would have to drive though all Saudi-controlled territory," Migos interjected.

"Driving through Saudi from the Oman border would be easier; the Saudis will be a lot less vigilant inside their own borders," Pat said.

"You mean we're in the wrong place," offered McDonald.

"Yeah, I think so. The CIA, CENTCOM and Clearwater are all trying to find the Iranians. Three of the four teams have already been found and destroyed. This last one is damn close to getting away," Pat said.

"What's the plan?" asked McDonald.

"Wait until the spooks find the bad guys. Then we either drive or fly to set up a blocking position," Pat said.

"I have some experience operating in Yemen. The Saudi border from the Red Sea until you get about one hundred or one hundred and fifty miles into the interior is very mountainous. Unless the Iranians move dismounted, they won't be able to cross in the mountains. If the selection criteria for where they breach is Houthi-controlled and open desert, that leaves a stretch that's only about one hundred miles long," Jankowski said.

Pat went to the truck and returned with a road map. While the guys continued to grill, eat and talk, he studied the map.

"If you have to breach the border east of the mountains and limit yourself to Houthi-controlled areas, that restricts you to only one road within Yemen." Pat laid the map on the ground and pointed.

"This road from Khbash in Saudi is the only road. I don't know what the desert looks like and I don't know what the Iranians are driving. I doubt they would want to remain off-road very long. My guess is they'll cross within twenty miles of this road on the side closest to Oman," Pat added.

"You think we should relocate into Yemen and catch them after they breach the fence line?" McDonald said.

"Yeah, I doubt we would get permission to do anything on the Saudi side. Yemen is the Wild West. We can do anything we want on that side," Pat said.

"Are we going to fly in?" asked Migos.

"Yeah," Pat said.

"If you do that, you stand to lose a very expensive airplane. The Houthis have handheld SAMs, SA-7s and 12.7mm Dushkas. They've taken out a lot of Saudi and Emirati aircraft," Jankowski said.

"We just need to find a remote spot with a dirt airstrip. Are there any chutes in the plane?" Pat asked.

"Yeah, four of them."

"We can do a mini JCT. Send four guys down first by parachute to clear the runway and make sure there are no hostiles with SAMs."

"You're having Ranger flashbacks."

"It's the old drill. The jump clearing team goes first, the plane goes second, and once we're on the ground, we drop ramp and drive off with the vehicles," Pat said.

"Let's get the Flyers loaded back onto the aircraft. We need to set up the satcom to download the terrain data we'll need to find a spot where we can land. We also need current satellite images to confirm Houthi and Saudi positions. I'll talk with David Forrest and Mike Guthrie. It would help a lot if we could get a dedicated UAV," Pat said.

The team got up and went to work. Migos took an e-tool and threw sand onto the fire. In seconds the small camp was gone, and the men were moving.

"What are you going to do with that Explorer, boss?" asked Migos.

"I'm going to have to leave it."

"Better hope the Bedouins don't find it."

Chapter 12

Thablotin, Saudi Arabia

Colonel Shalmani ordered the driver to stop at the gas station in the village of Thablotin. The sun was beginning to dip over the massive sand dunes that surrounded the village.

He had changed the plan when they'd reached the midway point. He was anxious and felt much safer moving than hiding out in Oman, waiting for night to fall. Ever since deciding to drive through the day and not stop at Haima, he had been studying his map, working to find the perfect crossing point. He'd finally settled on Thablotin. The remote area, combined with the terrain that masked movement, made the fence line five miles east of Thablotin a good place to cross into Saudi Arabia.

The nine Iranians had been alternating navigating, driving and sleeping. Halfway through the trip, with another six hundred miles to cover, Colonel Shalmani was feeling cramped from sitting. He got out to stretch his legs and to pay the gas station attendant. He spoke in an Iraqi dialect of Arabic and he was careful to speak very little when dealing with the Pakistani cashier.

Inside the gas station was a small grill, and Colonel Shalmani bought plates of chicken biryani for his men. Outside the gas station were picnic tables where the men were sitting and smoking. All of the weapons were concealed inside the two Land Cruisers. The driver of each vehicle remained with the vehicle just in case.

After delivering the food, he updated the men on the plan. "The route will be all unpaved side roads for the next three hundred and fifty miles, until we reach Highway 180 in Al-Kharkir. We will refuel at there and then travel on Highway 180 until we reach Sharurah. From there, we will continue west from on Highway 15 for three hundred kilometers and camp east of Khbash, on the flat plains just east of the mountains. When we are in the camp in Khbash, we'll radio to our Quds brothers, who will accompany our Houthi escort. We'll arrive at the camp in the late afternoon. Tomorrow evening we cut the fence and we will cross into Yemen. A Houthi element with Quds advisors will meet us after we have crossed into Yemen and escort us to Sana'a. The border crossing is in a contested area between the Saudis and the Houthis. Make sure you're ready for trouble."

Colonel Shalmani's men all nodded in assent. Sometimes it surprised him how rarely any of his man asked questions. Over the years, they had learned to trust him and follow his orders without ever challenging him. His record spoke for itself. That was why he'd received special attention from General Suleimani. His reputation was growing.

Chapter 13

Al-Baqa, Yemen

Pat stood on the open ramp of the C-130 between Burnia and Jankowski. The cold seeped through his heavy clothing. At ten thousand feet, he didn't need oxygen. His eyes were on Migos, who was serving in the role of jumpmaster. In the dim red-lit cabin, Pat could see Bill Sachse behind Migos. Beyond Sachse were the two Flyers, open-air tactical vehicles that resembled dune buggies. Roger McDonald was in the driver's seat of the lead Flyer, which was positioned in the center of the vehicle.

Migos motioned, giving the "move to the rear" command, and Pat moved to within one meter of the edge of the ramp. Migos then pointed out the door, giving the "go" command, and the three men simultaneously exited the aircraft facefirst.

Pat stabilized himself with his arms and legs spread-eagled as he free-fell into the night sky. He focused on locating the airstrip through the limited illumination. The lights from the village of Al-Baqa south of the airstrip were his only reference. He checked his altimeter at four thousand feet, and at three thousand feet, he pulled the ripcord, deploying his RAM-1 parachute. Guided by the village lights, he was able to locate the three-thousand-foot airstrip. He flared his parachute and landed at the near end of the dirt runway.

After releasing his parachute and stuffing it in a bag to keep it from getting sucked up by the C-130's turbine engines, Pat removed three boxes of IR ChemLites from his pack. He snapped each of the thirty ChemLites and began his survey of the airfield. He dropped a bundle of five lights wrapped in an elastic band at his feet and then made his way down the runway at a slow jog. Every thirty steps, which was about every fifty meters, he dropped a ChemLite in the center of the runway. In some places, sand drifts encroached onto the runway, so Pat checked each one to make sure the wheels would be clear of them and the wings and propellers were elevated enough to avoid trouble. When he reached the end of the runway, he dropped what lights remained in a bundle and pressed the push-to-talk button on his radio.

"Hercules, this is Walsh. Airfield is clear, over," Pat said. "Burnia and Jankowski, report."

From an overwatch position between the village and the airfield, Burnia surveyed the village from high ground with his Accuracy International AX 338 sniper rifle. "This is Burnia. I'm set, area is clear."

From a position on the hills west of the airfield, Jankowski surveyed the flat open terrain around the airfield. "This is Jankowski. Set, area is clear."

"Hercules, you are clear to land."

The Hercules had been doing racetracks at ten thousand feet. Once the command to land was given, the pilots put the plane into a steep corkscrew descent. The onboard navigation system accurately brought the aircraft to the edge of the runway.

The pilot wore night vision goggles. Once he spotted the first ChemLite bundle, he adjusted the altitude and planted the wheels three hundred feet past the edge of the runway. As soon as the plane touched the runway, the pilot reversed thrust by changing the propeller pitch. The restraining straps on the cargo and the passengers strained as the aircraft came to an abrupt halt.

Pat stepped in front and ground-guided the aircraft to the wider end of the runway, where it had room to turn around by pivoting. Once the aircraft was pointed back down the runway in the direction from where it had come, which was north, away from the village, the rear cargo door dropped. The two General Dynamics Flyers bounded down the ramp and pulled to a sliding halt fifty meters from the aircraft. Pat gave the loadmaster Bill Sachse a thumbs-up signal, and seconds later the ramp closed and the Hercules engines revved.

The pilot released the brake, and the plane sped down the pitch-black runway. Using the NVGs to stay in the center of the narrow strip marked by IR ChemLites, the pilot lifted the plane into the night sky. The crew was aware that an Apache had been shot down in Al-Baqa only months previously, so the climb beyond handheld surface-to-air missile range was a nail biter; the villagers had definitely been awoken by the noise. With Mike Guthrie's assistance, the plane was able to cross back into Saudi airspace on its way to Al Dhafra Air Force Base in UAE.

Burnia and Jankowski converged on the two Flyer 72 vehicles parked at the edge of the runway, oriented north toward Saudi Arabia. Roger McDonald drove one vehicle and Migos the other. The Flyers were unusually designed Special Operations light tactical vehicles with no doors and no roof. The roll bars and most of the vehicles' construction were steel tubing. A ring mount in the center directly behind the driver's head hosted a M230LF 30mm chain gun with an advanced fire control system that included a cooled thermal system with a range of up to twenty kilometers. The M230 was capable of hitting point targets at three thousand meters with high-explosive dual-purpose rounds. With a firing rate of two hundred rounds per minute, the 30mm chain gun had some serious firepower.

Jankowski was in the turret behind McDonald in the first vehicle, and Burnia manned the gun behind Migos in the second. Riding shotgun next to Migos, Pat toggled the push-to-talk switch on his comm set and gave the order to move out to the blocking position.

Pat noticed the satphone he had placed on the shelf in front of him was ringing. He had to remove his helmet and headset to take the call.

"This is Pat."

"I found your target," said David Forrest in his British accent.

"How…where?" asked Pat.

"We got some help from an EC-130 Compass Call aircraft working a counterterror mission for JSOC in your area. They monitored a UHF radio call between what we think are your Iranians and what we believe is a Quds unit working with a Houthi element. They've proposed a linkup fifteen kilometers west of Al-Baqa, at the entrance to a mountain pass. I'll send you the coordinates."

"Do we have time? Where are the Iranians?"

"Still north of the border inside Saudi. West of Khbash. They're on the move, and depending on the speed of travel, they'll arrive at the linkup point within the next one to two hours," David said.

"What about the Houthi element?"

"They're inside the mountains, roughly two miles from the entrance point of the pass."

"Any idea of the size and composition?" Pat asked.

"The intercept reported that the Iranians will have two SUVs and the Houthis will have four trucks. The signal is two flashes on the headlights for a challenge and three on the response."

"Great work, Dave, send me the location."

Pat immediately dialed Mike Guthrie.

"Dave Forrest just called. An ELINT bird picked up the Iranians coordinating the linkup for safe passage with the Houthis. It's close to our location in Al-Baqa. If I can get eyes on the linkup, can you get CAS? We should be able to take both forces out with one strike."

"How big a force are we talking about?" asked Mike.

"Iranians are in two SUVs and the Houthis are linking up with four trucks—technicals. They'll probably have more combat power in reserve."

"What do you have for combat power?" Mike asked.

"Five guys, two Flyer 72s with 30mm chain guns, plus M203s and a couple of sniper rifles."

"I want you to take them out with direct fire. We badly need an Iranian prisoner."

"Bombing them with an F-16 is a lot less risky. Why is direct fire worth it?" Pat asked.

"The new sultan is having legitimacy issues. The support from the Omani population is shaky. Having an Iranian to display to the crowd will give him the evidence he needs to show the Iranians were responsible and demonstrate that he did something about it."

"I imagine that would push the people toward Saudi and the US too."

"Yeah, it would, which is not a bad thing," David agreed.

"We'll try to grab one of the Persians. Can you get me some air support, just in case things go pear-shaped? Compass Call only supports SOCOM, which I'm guessing means they have operators nearby, which should also mean they have an AC-130 gunship in the area."

"Let me see what I can do. Send me your radio freq and a call sign, so if I get someone, you can talk."

"Great."

"Keep me posted."

"Wilco," Pat said.

Pat's vehicle led, with McDonald's trailing through the open desert. The silhouettes of the mountains on the horizon were ominous through his night vision goggles. They reached a massive mountainous wall, and Pat directed Migos to traverse it to the right. Eventually they reached the tip of a huge rocky finger. Pat stopped the convoy and went to the hood of the vehicle, waving everyone over.

Once the five men were gathered, he walked forward to the very edge of the fingertip, where it became possible to see to the west.

"This is a great vantage point. Five kilometers due north is the fence that separates Yemen and Saudi. Sometime in the next thirty to ninety minutes, our targets are going to cut through that fence line and drive in this direction." Pat showed them a tablet with the map data and a blue dot showing their location for effect.

"If you look due west, you can see that big bowl surrounded on three sides by mountains. If you look at this map, there's a narrow gap big enough to allow vehicle traffic to pass. A Houthi element of four vehicles is going to come out of that pass and link up with the Iranians after they pass into Yemen from Saudi." The men switched back and forth from using their night vision goggles to see the terrain to removing them to check the tablet for the map data.

"Now comes the hard part. Mike wants an Iranian prisoner. When the four Houthi vehicles are outside the pass, and once both Iranian SUVs are inside the bowl, we're going to engage. We're going to kill everyone in the lead Iranian vehicle and every one of the Houthis, but we're going to disable the trail Iranian vehicle and then move in and grab one of the Iranian Revolutionary Guard personnel to bring back to Oman as a trophy."

"Boss, the Houthis will cover the bowl from the high ground. We're going to face more than just the six vehicles," Jankowski said.

"I'm trying to get air support. Once we trip the ambush, we need a SPECTRE gunship or attack air to kill everything south of the linkup point so we can focus on everything else," Pat said.

"How's that coming along?" Migos asked.

"Mike is working on it."

"How do we disable the trail Iranian SUV?" Burnia asked.

"We'll move into defilade positions along this ridge, looking down into the bowl. Once the two elements get within one hundred meters of each other, Jankowski and Burnia will engage the four Houthi vehicles and the lead Iranian vehicle. Engaging with the 30mms at a range of two kilometers, that should be quick. I'll take the .338 and move forward another klick, and while the big guns are taking out the other vehicles, I'll shoot the driver and pin down the trail vehicle. Once your fight is over, both Flyer vehicles will advance, and we'll deal with the three to four survivors of the trail vehicle and grab one of them as a prisoner."

"That's pretty crazy," Migos said.

"I'm open to suggestions, but remember, we don't have much time."

"What will we do if we don't get air support?" asked McDonald.

"Mike said he would try, which means that there's a ninety-five percent chance," said Pat.

"Yeah, but if?" said Migos.

"Then we won't assault through. We'll kill all of them from standoff, outside their range, and then we'll withdraw and exfil. The Houthi trucks are technicals. They'll have 12.7mm machine guns in the back of the pickups, but no night vision.

They can't hit us at two kilometers. They won't even see us," Pat said.

Burnia spoke up for the first time. "I'm good with that." The rest of the team grunted their assent. Pat removed the sniper case from the Flyer cab, assembled the weapon and grabbed a poncho liner and his satphone.

"You guys better move into position. I'll make sure you can see me from the ridge. I'm sure the Iranians will have night vision, so I won't mark my position. Make sure you put glint on your helmets. When Mike comes through with the air support, we don't want any issue with positive ID from air force."

Pat walked with the .338 PSR at the ready. It was a cool night; the ground was rocky. He occasionally stumbled when the toe of his boot caught a rock. He walked downhill toward the bowl for fifteen minutes. All he could hear was the wind as he lay down in a small depression and set up his weapon. The Oasys Thermal gave him a range out to two thousand meters. The AI .338 Lapua was a bolt-action rifle that weighed seventeen pounds and had recorded kills beyond two thousand meters. However, with the wind, at night, shooting from elevation against a fast-moving target who would probably be surrounded by dust from the lead vehicle, Pat felt a lot more comfortable making the shot at one thousand meters.

Lost in the preparation, Pat almost missed the radio call that would have been coming across all of the team radios.

"Houston six, this is Ghost Rider. Houston, this is Ghost Rider."

"Ghost Rider, Houston," Pat responded.

"We're on station over your position. I have a fix on two vehicles, with two pax per and a dismount one kilometer to the north," said Ghost Rider.

"Do you want to confirm friendly?" replied Pat.

A sparkle of IR light from the sky blanketed the Flyers, and seconds later another sparkle hit Pat. "Confirmed friendly. Ghost Rider, can you scan south one to three klicks into the ravine, see if you can identify the bad guys?" Pat said.

Several minutes passed. Pat lay prone behind his rifle, scanning to the north toward the border with his thermals.

"Houston, we have identified nine vehicles that are halted approximately four kilometers south of your location," the voice said over the radio.

"Roger, four of those vehicles should be moving soon towards my location. Report when they do. Target the remaining vehicles and any dismounts that are probably moving into position on the ridgeline overwatching the bowl and my position. Once this thing goes hot, you can fire at will," said Pat.

"Wilco, Houston." The radio was silent for the next ten minutes. The cold was starting to bother Pat, so he wrapped the poncho liner around his body as he lay on the rocky ground.

"Two vehicles, due north, five kilometers, moving through the fence line," Jankowski said over the radio.

"Houston, this is Ghost Rider. Four vehicles on the move, heading your way."

"Roger, Ghost Rider." Pat was no longer cold. The adrenaline was surging through his body. He tried to steady his breathing.

"We have vehicle movement to the south, four technicals," said Burnia.

"When I give the order to fire, Burnia, you engage the technicals, and Jankowski, you fire on the lead Iranian SUV. I'll engage the trail, and Ghost Rider will take out the Houthi main body back inside the ravine," said Pat.

"Roger," said Jankowski.

"Roger," said Burnia.

"Ghost Rider standing by with 105mm at your command."

Pat watched the moving SUVs close with the technical trucks. He could only see one of the trucks. He watched it as it flicked its headlights twice to challenge the Iranians. The lead Iranian responded with three flashes. Pat tracked the second SUV through his thermals. He had a spot on the ground he was using as a reference point. He waited until the lead vehicle crossed the small rock outcropping before he gave the order to fire.

Oblivious to the explosions from the 30mm high-explosive rounds tearing through the Houthi and lead Iranian vehicle, Pat slowly squeezed the trigger and fired his first round into the driver's side of the trail SUV, through the windshield. Unable to see through the window, he continued to pump rounds into the cab of the SUV even after it had halted.

Pat could hear the 105mm cannon rounds exploding in the distance. Both 30mm chain guns were engaging the unarmored Houthi pickup trucks. The exploding HEDP rounds were devastating against the soft-skinned vehicles. Sporadic automatic AK fire was coming from the ridgeline near the entrance to the ravine.

"Ghost Rider, Houston. Enemy dismounts six hundred meters west of my position."

"Tallyho, Houston."

"Cleared hot," replied Pat.

A fusillade of 30mm cannon fire rained down on the twelve Houthi dismounts hiding from Burnia and Jankowski's lethal onslaught.

"Burnia, cover. Jankowski, move to my position." Pat dropped his goggles, stood and began to walk toward the SUVs. The lead SUV was fully engulfed in flames, while the trail vehicle appeared undamaged through his NVGs. By the time he was five hundred meters from the vehicle, Jankowski's Flyer was next to him. Pat substituted his sniper rifle for an M4 and continued his advance. When he got to within fifty meters of the SUV, automatic fire erupted from the front and back of the vehicle. Pat engaged immediately, and the burst of the M230 chain gun sent six 30mm high-explosive rounds into the SUV, turning it into a fireball. The bright flames interfered with his NVGs even though they were autogated.

"I have movement running from the truck," Jankowski replied.

"Don't shoot," Pat said as he raced around the truck. With the Flyer behind him, Pat ran after the figure, who was running toward the western edge of the bowl. The man ran with a limp and carried a rifle. Closer to the face the mountain, the bigger rocks and boulders made it impossible for the Flyer to follow. Pat chased the man as he wove his way between the boulders and steadily climbed. Pat continued to gain on the injured man. The man turned twice and fired bursts of automatic at Pat. After the third unaimed burst, Pat closed with the man.

With his weapon empty and without any spare magazines, The Quds soldier used his rifle like an ax and swung it down on Pat. Pat parried the swing with his own weapon, which he was carrying at port arms, and rushed into the Iranian. He dropped his head and crushed the Iranian's nose with his helmet, causing him to drop his rifle. Dropping his carbine, he grappled the man by the shoulders. Still standing, but barely conscious, the Iranian attempted to elbow Pat in the face in a drunken maneuver, but Pat stepped back and then dropped the Iranian with a right hook that connected with Shalmani's jaw.

Pat flex-cuffed the man with his hands behind his back and dragged him down the hill to the awaiting Flyer. He dumped the man in the well in the rear of the vehicle, making sure he was secured to the vehicle with an A7A strap. He then hopped into the right front seat, and they sped back to ridgeline, where McDonald and Burnia were still located.

"Ghost Rider, can you provide us overwatch while we cross back into Saudi?"

"Wilco, Houston."

"Let's go through the same gap in the fence as the Iranians came through and head back to Oman," Pat said.

"Are we going to go through gas stations like this?" Migos asked.

"Take the M230s apart. The Saudis will think we're extreme off-roaders or something. I'll call Mike, and he'll clear our passage with the Saudi government."

The trip through Saudi Arabia to the Oman border occurred without incident.

"When are we going to hand over the prisoner?" asked Migos through his comms system. The open-air Flyer was loud, and it was difficult to communicate without the headsets, which allowed the entire team to hear every conversation.

"We'll hand him off at the airfield. A Blackhawk will meet us once we get there," said Pat.

"What's the TOT on our ride out?" asked Migos.

"Two days without a shower and a couple thousand miles across the open desert, and you're ready to quit," Pat chided.

"Yeah, exactly. The seats on this thing are awesome. I wish we'd had these when I was on active duty. The problem is that guy in the backseat. He smells like a goat."

Migos was driving from the front center seat, with Jankowski to his left and Pat to his right. At the mention of the Quds prisoner, both Pat and Jankowski looked into the backseat. The prisoner lay blindfolded and gagged on his stomach, with his knees bent and his ankles flex-cuffed to his wrists. A single rope attached to the steel tubing above him was tied to his flex-cuffs. His face was covered with dried blood, and fresh blood seeped through the bandage that had been wrapped around his right leg, where he had received a laceration from the earlier action.

"According to the GPS, we have another ninety minutes to get to Al-Mazyunah. The Hercules and the Blackhawk helicopter will hopefully arrive soon after we get there. You'll be back in Abu Dhabi for dinner," Pat said.

"Do you plan on asking the Iranian any questions before we get rid of him?" Migos asked.

"No, Mike was pretty clear about that. The Agency is going to interrogate him and then hand him off to the Omanis. Besides, he doesn't have any answers I'm interested in hearing," asked Pat.

"You don't want to know why he torched the Chedi and killed everyone in it?" Migos said.

"I can tell he's the commander of the unit. There's no tactical reason to kill every person in the Chedi. He did it because he's a psychopath and that's what psychopaths do. No sense asking him about it."

"Do you want a few minutes with him for payback?" Migos asked.

"No, the CIA interrogators will be get the answers they need out of him. When they hand him over to the Omanis, he's going to wish I killed him."

"You think so?"

"Definitely. He's going to confess his sins on TV, and then he's going to have a very public and painful execution," Pat said.

"Sucks to be him. Once I get back to Abu Dhabi, I'm going to Dubai. I'm heading to the Cavalli Club to spend all that money we just made grabbing this sack of shit," Migos said.

McDonald's voice came over the net. "How much did we make?" he asked.

"The bonus on this job is one hundred and twenty-five thousand each. That assumes I get all this equipment back in one piece," Pat said.

Burnia's voice came over the net. "What time are you leaving for Dubai? I might want to come with you."

"I'll leave at ten. Be warned, I cannot spend all my time trying to convince some poor girl to hang with you. I have ladies who demand my full attention."

"I'm gonna come along. I think I want to see this," Jankowski said.

For the first time in days, Pat smiled. He liked that the team was bonding.

"What about you, boss? What are your plans?" Migos asked.

"I'll take that Explorer back to Muscat and return it. Hopefully they've relaxed the martial law enough to do that. Then I'll move the boat back to Abu Dhabi," Pat said.

"You need me to go with you. That's another six hours on the road at least," McDonald said over the radio.

"I'm good. I might need you in Dubai to look after these guys and keep them out of jail. Did you guys read the article about the Brit who got a three-year sentence for grabbing some guy's ass in a bar as a joke? Watch yourself. The Dubai court of first appeals is a scary place to be," Pat said.

When Pat arrived at the outskirts of Muscat, it was dark. What surprised him most was the lights. Somehow the Omanis had found a way to restore electricity to at least some of Muscat. He checked his phone and discovered cell phone service had also been restored. When he reached the first roadblock, he realized martial law was still in effect. Fortunately, he was able to call Colonel Al-Busaidi and gain permission to drive through.

The next day, he returned the rental first thing in the morning and was preparing the *Sam Houston* to sail when Walt Berg met him on the marina slipway.

"Getting ready to sail?" Walt said.

"Nothing left for me to do here. I stopped at the Chedi this morning. Not much progress in identifying the bodies," Pat said.

"It's going to take months."

"How's the new sultan doing? Does he have control of this beast yet?" asked Pat.

"It looks like he's going to make it through the transition. He's solidly pro-American, so we want to keep him around as long as possible."

"Let me know if anything develops at the Chedi. I'd like to give Susu a proper funeral," Pat said.

"I will. Take care of yourself," Walt said.

"Same to you."

The two men shook hands, and then Pat tossed the lines over the side into the *Sam Houston* and stepped on board through the side door.

Chapter 14

Abu Dhabi

It was midday when Pat backed the *Sam Houston* into its familiar slip in the Intercontinental Marina. The weather was unusually cloudy, and the temperature was a comfortable seventy-five degrees. It was the weekend and the marina was busy with activity. Many of the hotel patrons were dining outside at the hotel restaurants overlooking the marina.

While Pat hooked up the external power, he heard footsteps. He turned and saw his old friend Mike Guthrie. The two men shook hands, and Mike helped Pat hook up the water.

"Are you hungry?" Pat asked. "I could use some Belgian Café pork ribs."

"Yeah, but it has to wait. We need to talk inside, away from other ears."

Pat led Mike into the salon and the two men sat across from each other on opposite couches.

"The prisoner you grabbed is Colonel Shalmani from Quds. He led the attack against the Chedi. He's a sick son of a bitch."

"I figured as much."

"He turned into a real talker. He was willing to do anything to keep us from handing him over to the Omanis."

"I'm beyond revenge in this situation, Mike. I don't care what happens to some Iranian Revolutionary Guard peon."

"This is where it gets interesting. Do you remember last month when the Houthis claimed they shot a cruise missile at the UAE nuclear power plant?"

"Yeah. On the news, they said they missed. It was the same week that the missile they shot at the Saudi king's palace was knocked down by a Patriot missile."

"They did shoot at the nuclear plant. The missile hit the side of a mountain in Yemen."

"Okay, so what?"

"Shalmani and his Iranian team were the group who fired that missile, along with some Houthis. He's also the guy who sank the UAE frigate with another missile—not a cruise, just a surface-to-surface."

"I'm with you, go on."

"The Iranians have three more cruise missiles deployed to Yemen. The only reason they haven't fired them yet is that they realized they didn't have the correct topographical data after the first one crashed. These missiles skim the earth at high speed only a hundred meters above the ground. If you don't have the right topo data inputted, they hit mountains. When they do have the right topo data, it's almost impossible to shoot them down. They're so low, the terrain masks them from most air defense radar. The UAE doesn't have an air defense system that could stop them. Properly programmed, they'll reach the target."

"What would happen if they hit one of UAE's nuclear power plants?"

"The reactors are fueled. If they get hit, it's going to be a nuclear event. A major incident."

"What does that mean?"

"A nuclear cloud with a fallout radius of two to three hundred miles. Al Barakah is on the border with Saudi. If you draw a three-hundred-mile circle around it, then it includes Riyadh, Qatar, Dubai, the entire width of the Persian Gulf and even a small part of Iran."

"The ayatollahs believe in all that twelfth imam end-of-the-world stuff. What are the chances the Iranians can fix the remaining missiles?"

"They need to obtain the geospatial data and then they need to upload it into the flight program of each of the missiles."

"Which I assume the Iranians are doing."

"Yes, Shalmani confirmed that."

"Did he give you the location of the missiles?"

"No, he didn't have them. He was only given the info on the missile he launched unsuccessfully."

"Now what?"

"We're scouring Yemen for the missiles. But they have a lot of very big caves in those mountains, and we don't think we're going to be able find them until they're taken out for launch, which is going to be too late."

"So, let me guess. This is where I come in."

"Exactly, we need you to find the missiles."

"How much time is there? How long will it take for them to get the terrain data and input it?"

"We don't know. They've had over a month, and it could take days or even months. The level of detail on the geospatial data they need is not easy to get. The US doesn't have it for every place on earth. We don't have it for every area in Yemen. Iran doesn't have any satellites, so they would need help, probably from the Russians."

"Why would the Russians help the Iranians irradiate the Persian Gulf?"

"Are you kidding? Do you have any idea what that would do to the price of oil? It would instantly fix their economy. They're the number one producer of oil in the world."

"Twenty percent of the world's oil goes through the gulf, but that also includes Iranian oil. Why would they be that stupid?"

"You need to keep up with the rebirth of the Persian empire. The Iranians can move oil through Iraq and Syria all the way to the Mediterranean. They don't need the Persian Gulf nearly as much as their enemies do."

"What do you want me to do?"

"Go back into Yemen. Find those missiles and destroy them."

"That's all?"

"I'll give your guy at Clearwater everything he could possibly want from the sky. We have our own people working on the same thing. Between the two of them, we should have that side of things covered. What's going to be needed is someone on the ground."

"Okay, I'll get started after lunch. I'm really hungry, can we go now?"

"Pork ribs."

"Pork ribs and Chimay Blue beer, it's amazing."

"Should you be drinking before undertaking dangerous clandestine operations?"

"The pork ribs are served with a sauce made with Leffe Belgian Blonde. Are you recognizing a theme here?"

"I'm wondering how seriously you're taking this assignment."

"Very, but it's going to take a day or two of prep. If you have the info on where the last cruise missile was launched from, that will serve as my starting point."

"I'll get that to you soonest."

"Now let's go partake of the fruits of the Trappist monks. As Ben Franklin said, 'Beer is proof that God loves us and want us to be happy.'"

Pat and Mike sat at an outside table that overlooked the marina. The *Sam Houston* was the largest boat. It was a Friday afternoon, and the British brunch crowd was just getting started at the Yacht Club restaurant and club, next door to the Belgian Café. Young expat men and woman were already on the outside dance floor. The Friday brunches in UAE were all-you-can-eat-and-drink affairs, and usually by five in the afternoon, things got a little sloppy. It was early yet, and the DJ was playing top forties, the crowd still looking smart and elegant.

"Now that you've had a few minutes to think about it, what's your plan?" Mike asked.

"I'll need you to talk with the crown prince for me. The best way to get in country will be by boat from Assab, Eritrea. It's about thirty miles across the gulf to Yemen from Assab. That part of the coast is where the fighting is now taking place between the UAE and the Houthis." He paused to drink his beer.

"Cruise missiles are big. The trucks that move them must be sixteen wheelers. In that part of Yemen, not many roads into the mountains will support anything that big. The Iranians only have two ways into Yemen. The first is along the south coast of Yemen, which is a good route for small stuff, but not feasible for cruise missiles. The second route is across the water from Djibouti, basically the same route as the Emirates are using, only thirty miles to the south."

"You're going to follow the route the missiles took."

"Exactly. All the way from the coast into the mountains, where I'm pretty sure they're hiding them in caves next to flat open areas suitable to launch them from."

"How are you going to track them?"

"You can't drive a big truck with a huge missile box on it without people noticing."

"Most likely these are Qader missiles that are designed as antiship cruise missiles."

"What's the range?"

"The extended version has a range of six hundred kilometers with a warhead of two hundred kilograms."

"Is that enough to punch through the dome of a nuclear reactor?"

"The kinetic force alone will punch through the dome; these missiles are designed to penetrate warships. If they're on target, they'll pass through and detonate the reactor core."

"Back to the plan. With that range, the launch site is going to have to be on the eastern edge of the Houthi-controlled area of Yemen. East of Sana'a. They're probably storing them somewhere further to the west in a safe zone. Al-Hudaydah is the port city where all the fighting between the UAE and Houthis is going on. The Houthis own it and the UAE is trying to capture it. Most likely the missiles were offloaded in Al-Hudaydah, so that's where I'll start."

"That's the plan?"

"Yup, unless David Forrest or one of your analyst groups finds the missiles from the air."

"What are you going to do once you find the missiles?"

"Airstrike would be my first choice. Second choice is demo."

"I'll make sure we have something on standby."

"Make sure they have BLU-109s or something with penetration power. We might have to punch through some mountain or bunker to get to them."

"Will do."

"Who are you taking with you?" asked Mike.

"I'll do the recon part alone. As I find each missile, I'll put a guy in overwatch with a JTAC system."

"How's your Arabic?"

"Not great. Barely conversational, but good enough. I'll get by."

"So that's the plan?"

"Yup. How many other teams do you have doing the same thing?"

"JSOC has several teams of operators in the search. I have every Agency asset in Yemen on it as well."

"Why even call me in, then?"

"None of those guys have your record when it comes to tracking things down. At the moment, you're my best hope."

"I'll try not to disappoint. Can we eat now?"

Chapter 15

Al-Hudaydah, Yemen

Pat drove a black Kawasaki 250 KLR motorcycle off the amphibious landing craft and onto the beach. He had been traveling all day. The first leg of his journey was the daily shuttle from Al Dhafra Air Force Base in Abu Dhabi to Assab, Eritrea, in a C-17 cargo jet. The second leg was a two-hour crossing of the Red Sea in a flat-bottomed landing craft that had the worst stability at sea Pat had ever experienced. Despite the mild weather, it was not a pleasant crossing. Several of the soldiers assigned to an 8x8 Patria combat vehicle that had crossed with him had become violently sick.

The stretch of beach the craft landed on was twelve miles south of Al-Hudaydah. The terrain was a flat, dusty desert with hardly any vegetation. Fifteen miles to the east, he could see the mountains. The green on the mountain foothills provided a contrast to the bleak brown dustbowl he was currently in. Thirty miles beyond the gateway to the mountains was the city of Sana'a, the capital of Yemen and headquarters of the Houthi rebel government. He was in the most contested area of Yemen, but at the moment it felt peaceful.

As he drove his motorcycle north along Route 60, the coastal road, he began to see Yemenis. Emaciated figures were picking through the occasional piles of trash left by Emirati military units, searching for valuable brass ammunition casings and other useful items. The sun was beginning to set over the Red Sea to his left. He came upon a military unit in an assembly area. Arrayed in a in big circle were fourteen Leclerc tanks along with a larger assortment of Cayenne MRAPs, Oshkosh MATVs and NIMR 4x4 wheeled vehicles. He drove his bike unchallenged into the middle of the circle. The soldiers and crews manning the vehicles remained unseen.

Pat removed his motorcycle helmet and placed it on the backpack that was tied down to the rear of the bike. He wore gray Patagonia tactical pants and a black Marmot jacket. Underneath his jacket was a small Tyr nylon plate carrier with a combination of soft armor and a ceramic plate for extra protection. He pulled down the black bandana he was using to protect his nose and mouth from the dust and walked to a gathering of ten to twelve people collected in the center of the circle.

Their Arabic was loud and harsh, which could only mean it was either an argument or a negotiation. Only two people were doing the talking. One was wearing a desert camouflage uniform, with an Emirati Armed Forces symbol and a star on the rank tab in front of his jacket, symbolizing the rank of lieutenant colonel. The other person appeared to be an elderly Yemeni civilian. The Yemeni wore a brown sports jacket over a beige dishdasha. He had an off-white headdress, and stuck inside a belt worn high over his midsection, he had a large curved dagger in a green scabbard. Nobody greeted Pat or paid him any attention as he infiltrated the gathering. All eyes were on the two men who were loudly and aggressively going back and forth.

Pat couldn't understand every word, but he caught enough to confirm it was a negotiation. When the two men reached an agreement, a junior officer, a captain with three stars on his desert camouflage uniform, handed a stack of cash to a lieutenant, who in turn handed it off to the Yemeni. The junior office then led the Yemeni and his six similarly dressed cohorts over to a section of Oshkosh MATV four-wheeled combat vehicles.

"*Salaam alaikum*," Pat said to the lieutenant colonel as soon as he was able to get his attention.

"*Wa alaikum salaam.*"

Pat removed a document from the interior of his jacket and handed it to the officer, who reflexively took it. The letter was in Arabic, signed by the UAE's crown prince. The officer studied the letter for several minutes and then handed the document back to Pat.

"How can I help you?" the lieutenant colonel said in English.

"My name is Pat Walsh. I'm going to drive to Sana'a tonight on my bike, and I was hoping to get an intelligence update from you before I go."

"I'm Colonel Marwan. We'll provide you any assistance we can, but traveling to Sana'a is not possible. The route is not yet clear."

"I understand. But I would really appreciate it if we could go to a map and someone could point out where all the good guys and bad guys are."

The lieutenant colonel signaled for Pat to follow and led him to a small tent next to a lone Leclerc tank parked in the center of the assembly area.

Inside the tent, the two men sat in field chairs, on opposite sides of a table that held a map board. A Pakistani servant poured the two men tea.

"We're here," said Lieutenant Colonel Marwan, pointing out a location on the acetate-covered map below Al-Hudaydah with a pencil. "Twelve kilometers due north is Al-Hudaydah. To get to Sana'a, you must first get north of Al-Hudaydah. The city is heavily defended by Houthis. All the roads entering it are mined. The harbor is even mined. The road to Al-Hudaydah will not be cleared for many days."

"What about if I go around the city to the east?"

"That's why I was talking to that tribal chief. The only way to bypass Al-Hudaydah is to travel ten kilometers to the east through the village of Marawi," Lieutenant Colonel Marwan, said placing his pencil on the village.

"That tribal chief was paid three days ago to seize Marawi. There is a deep wadi that extends from Marawi all the way to the base of the mountains. To gain the flank of Al-Hudaydah, we must first have Marawi. The tribal chief took our money. He asked for additional vehicles and weapons and we provided them. Then, instead of taking Marawi as he promised, he returned today to ask for more," he said with an expression of disbelief.

"He claims the Houthis stole his vehicles and that he needs money to buy them back. He said he needs more vehicles because the enemy in Marawi is big in number," the lieutenant colonel said.

"You have to pay the Yemenis to fight?"

"Yes, only they don't fight. They're thieves. We pay them in equipment and money to fight. They turn around and pay the Houthis in equipment and money to retreat. Sometimes the local tribes give the territory back to the Houthis, just so they can come back to us and get paid again. Yemenis are greedy. Sheikh Mohammed, he paid all the major tribal elders, but the money didn't flow down to the little chiefs, like the man you just saw, and now we must pay again. It's a very unfair situation," Lieutenant Colonel Marwan said with disgust.

"To get on this road that starts in Hamadryad and leads into the mountains, I'll need to get very close to Marawi. If I do that, are the Houthis in Marawi going to shoot at me?" Pat said, pointing to a road on the map beyond Marawi.

"Yes, they'll kill you. You'll be in their range. They have at least two of our MATVs with 12.7mm remote weapon stations."

"When is your tribal elder going to attack Marawi or negotiate the handover?"

"He'll attack tomorrow morning. That is, unless he gets a better offer from the Houthis."

"What about beyond Marawi going east? Do you know where the enemy is over here toward the mountains?"

"There's a deep wadi that makes vehicle traffic impassible between the mountains and Marawi. There were two bridges across the wadi, but both have been destroyed. The only option to get to the mountain road is to first go through either Marawi or Hudaydah."

"Are you the lead element of the UAE Land Force?"

"Yes, there are no friendly forces north of this location."

"Thanks for the briefing, sir. I wish you luck in the days ahead."

When Pat left the tent, it was ten degrees cooler and completely dark. He returned to his bike and made a phone call to David Forrest at Clearwater.

"Do you have any updates?"

"Yes, I've been using that data the Emirati's gave you. Based on what you told me, I made the assumption that the Houthis were incapable of complex combat operations without the involvement of the Iranian Revolutionary Guard," Dr. Forrest answered in his professorial British tone.

"I'm with you so far."

"Then I plotted all the Houthi combat operations that met the criteria for complex offensive operations. I focused the collection systems around the areas for those operations. Eventually, the system identified the locations where we have a very high confidence level that you'll find Quds teams operating.

"We then eliminated the geographic areas that would put the UAE nuclear facilities outside of Iranian cruise missile range. We were left with only two locations."

"What are they?" Pat asked.

"Yazel and Shibam. I just sent you a message with the locations. If the missiles disembarked from the Port of Hudaydah, they'll have gone east to get within range of UAE. The Quds elements in those two villages are going to have knowledge of where they are."

"That's good work. Now I just need to find those Quds fellas and ask 'em."

"Godspeed."

Pat snapped on a pair of night vision goggles to his helmet mount and pulled on a pair of Oakley combat gloves over his hands. He opened the zipper in his jacket to give him quick access to the Glock 19 he was carrying in a shoulder holster attached to his plate carrier. He popped on the IR headlight and headed out cross-country, due east towards the mountains. With a dirt bike, he was pretty sure he could find a way in and out of the wadi even if the colonel was correct and the two bridges crossing the wadi East of Mahawi were knocked out.

It was four in the morning by the time Pat pulled the bike off the road five kilometers west of Yazel. The hardest part of the trip had been the last twenty kilometers, when he was descending the mountain. The road was steep and switchbacked. It would have been very slow going, moving a truck carrying a cruise missile over such a road. Pat covered the bike with camouflage netting. He removed a poncho liner and his sleeping bag from his pack and threw it down under a section of camouflage netting. The rushing of a waterfall was the only sound he could hear. He was surrounded by trees in an area that looked untraveled by humans.

Pat woke six hours later. After wolfing down an MRE, he climbed up the embankment, walked onto the road and started the trek toward Yazel. As he walked the mountain road, he would occasionally find a vantage point where he could see the village. The community was laid out in five different clusters of ten to twenty structures that all appeared to be precariously clinging onto the mountain. Around some of the clusters were beautifully terraced fields bordered by small trees.

When Pat entered the village, the streets were empty of people. Afternoon prayer had just begun. The telltale minarets of the mosque provided a guidepost to where he hoped to find the market and people.

Next to the mosque were a handful of storefronts and the first cars he had seen that day. The vehicles were all older-model Japanese and American pickups and SUVs. Outside one of the stores, he found a man baking bread in a wood-burning oven located, concentrating on flipping the round flat Arabic bread with a long wooden spatula that required both hands to operate.

Pat walked up to him and, after the traditional Arabic greeting, he asked the man for directions to the Persians (*alfuras alfarisia*). The man looked at him suspiciously. Most likely he had never before left this village and had never encountered an American. Unable to comprehend the threat from a lone Anglo deep in the Houthi tribal lands, the man eventually concluded Pat was working with the Persians and finally gave a response.

It took a long time with his broken Arabic, but eventually, Pat was on his way with directions. He was directed to a cluster of five buildings constructed on a steep mountainside. The walk up to the first building was taxing, and Pat was a little winded when he reached the door.

Unlike the rest of the sleepy village, the door opened as he approached and a man sporting an AK-74 stood behind it. Pat put up his hands and began his pitch in Arabic.

"I'm with the *New York Times*. I'm writing a story on the war. Please, I just want to ask some questions."

The man yelled out for someone more senior to come over.

When the commander arrived, the man holding the gun stepped forward out of the doorway to make room for his boss. When he took his eyes off Pat to negotiate the step, Pat drew his pistol from the shoulder holster and shot him in the face. Before the first man could fall, Pat shot the second man twice in the chest, then took the AK-74 from the dead man lying on the porch and entered the house.

He found a man rushing into the hallway holding a rifle and dropped him with the AK as soon as he came into view. The next men came from outside the house. Pat figured some of the Quds must have been staying in the building next door. Pat shot one man through the window as he was negotiating the low wall that separated the two buildings. While the Quds forces in the building next door were figuring out what to do, Pat went up the stairs and began to clear the second floor.

With the appropriated AK-74 rifle slung over his shoulder, Pat went room to room with his pistol drawn. The second floor was dark. As he opened the door to the third bedroom, shots went through the door and wooden splinters stung his face. He stepped behind the heavy wall while the Iranian pumped a magazine on full auto through the door. Hoping the man was changing magazines during a pause in firing, he opened the door, stepped into the bedroom and shot the man twice with his 9mm. He finished clearing the second floor and then took the stairs to the third.

He figured that by now, the remainder of the team from the adjacent building must have made it to his building. The third floor consisted of a single apartment, and it was empty. Looking out the window towards the street, it appeared clear. Careful not to expose himself, he checked the windows on the other three sides and spotted a man in a sniper position, aiming into the house from the building directly in the back.

He waited at the top of the stairs for the men to clear the first and then the second floor. When he heard footsteps on the stairwell, he picked up a heavy ceramic ashtray and held it in his left hand with the pistol in his right. With his back to the wall, he waited. He could hear two men advancing up the steps, moving slowly and stealthily. He held his breath as he watched the muzzle of an AK enter from the stairway.

When you enter a room, you can look right, center or left, but you can't simultaneously look in all three directions. If the lead man came in looking right, Pat was dead. Fortunately, the Iranian commando crossed the threshold into the room looking away from him. As the man's head swiveled to cover the right side of the room, Pat smashed the ashtray into the man's temple. As soon as the ashtray connected, he fired his pistol blindly into the stairwell. He heard the second man fall down the stairs. Pat stood in the doorway and shot the wounded man on the landing as he was trying to get up.

From a cargo pocket, he removed a set of flex-cuffs and tape and secured his prisoner. He still had the sniper to worry about. He grabbed the prisoner from the strap on the back of his body armor vest and dragged him down both sets of stairs. Fortunately, neither stairway had a window exposing him to the sniper. Once he reached the first floor, the only exposure would be when he tried to reach the pickup truck parked in front of the house.

He retraced his steps and searched the pockets of the dead Quds commandos for keys to the Toyota Hilux parked in front. After he checked the prisoner, he began to search the hallway. He slapped his head when he saw the keys were on top of the table closest to the entryway. With his prisoner under control and the keys in his hand, the next task was getting into the truck without being shot.

Despite the added weight, he left the body armor on the prisoner and lifted him on his back in a fireman's carry. The distance from the house to the truck was twenty meters. If the sniper hadn't moved, Pat would be obscured by the house and the trip would be safe. If the sniper had moved to a position that covered the front, Pat was a goner. He decided to get it over with quickly.

The twenty meters took an eternity. The strain of lifting a one-hundred-and-seventy-pound man wearing twenty pounds of equipment made Pat's chest pound. He opened the driver's-side door with the prisoner still on his back and then dumped the prisoner and pushed him over to the passenger side. He jumped into the truck, started it, hit the gas and sped off, waiting for a sniper shot.

The exit through the village was surprisingly unopposed. The Iranians must have done a lot of target practice, because there was no alarm from the gunfire. He pulled a bandana over his face and put on a pair of sunglasses to hide his Anglo features.

When he reached the turnoff where he'd left his bike, he stopped, opened the passenger door and dumped the now-conscious prisoner onto the side of the road. A short distance away, he found a big dropoff where he could dump the truck, and he sent it off into a deep crevasse He returned to the prisoner and dragged him down to his campsite, propping him up against a tree.

The man had a huge bruise on the side of his head from where the ashtray had hit him. Pat removed his knife and peeled the duct tape off the man's mouth.

"Do you speak Arabic?" he asked in Arabic. The man did not respond.

"Do you speak English?" he asked in English. The man did not respond.

"Some people think torture doesn't work. But those are people who've never tried it. Torture works. Not some of the time. It works all the time. What's going to happen next is that

I'm going to go for a walk down to that lake where you hear the waterfall. When I come back, you're going to tell me what you know about the location of the cruise missiles.

"While I'm gone, you can figure out how many times I'm going to have to waterboard you and how man body parts I need to cut off to get the information I need. Rest assured, whether you make this easy or hard on yourself, in the end, you will answer." Pat made the threat first in Arabic and then again in English.

He returned the duct tape to the man's mouth and tied a length of parachute cord to the flex-cuffs that bound the man's hands behind his back. He tossed the cord over a tree limb and pulled it until the increased tension forced the man onto the tips of his toes to avoid the pain from his shoulders. Lastly, he went over to his backpack and withdrew two three-gallon collapsible water containers.

The hike down to the lake with the waterfall was treacherous. He returned an hour later soaked with sweat. The two water containers were full, and his hands were aching. It was getting late in the afternoon, and Pat had not eaten, so he cooked an MRE next to his sleeping bag within sight of the prisoner.

When he finished, he walked over to the prisoner. The man's face was red, and his legs were shaking. Pat positioned the water containers and withdrew a towel from his bag before cutting the man down from the limb. He laid the man faceup, head down on the slope of the hill, tore the duct tape off the man's mouth and started to secure the towel around the man's face.

"I know where the trucks are," the man said in English.

"I hope you're telling the truth. If I go there and I don't find the trucks, things will go very bad for you," Pat said.

"My team was responsible for scouting the locations, and we emplaced all four trucks. I know where they are."

Pat went to his bike and returned with a map.

"Show me."

When he was done explaining how and where they had hidden the trucks, Pat shot the man in the head. He would have liked to let him go as a reward for cooperation, but if he did, he risked compromising the mission.

His next call was to Roger McDonald. The call after that was to Mike Guthrie.

"I think I have a fix on the missiles," Pat said.

"That was quick."

"I found a cooperative Iranian Revolutionary Guard who claims his team did the scouting and even escorted the trucks to the hide sites."

"How confident are you he wasn't lying?"

"Seventy, maybe eighty percent. Confident enough to dispatch the team. I have four sites and four men with JTAC gear."

"Send me the locations. If we can ID them from the air, we can take them out without having to put anyone on the ground."

"That won't work. They're in caves, under big hills. You're not going to be able to do the terminal guidance from the sky, and you're going to need special payloads."

"How deep are we talking?"

"Hundreds of feet, worst case."

"That'll take a MOP."

"What's that?"

"Massive ordnance penetrator. It's designed to penetrate deep earth. It's a thirty-ton warhead, and only a B-2 can deliver it."

"Is it guided by GPS or laser?"

"Laser. It'll need either a FAC-A or a JTAC."

"What do you want me to do with my guys?"

"Get them in place. Try to confirm your information before we bomb anything."

"I'll work to confirm and emplace the JTACs, you get the B-2s locked and loaded."

"How much time do you need for the JTACs?"

"They can insert tonight. It won't take them long to set up once they get on the ground."

"What about confirmation?"

"I'll work that tonight."

"Anything else?"

"We'll need persistent surveillance on each site before my guys insert. First, to make sure they go in clean. Second, so we can react in case I spook them tonight and they try to move the missiles."

"We'll put UAV coverage over all four possible sites, even though one of them no longer has a missile. If they try to move, the Reapers will take them out with Hellfire."

"I'll report when the JTACs are set and when I get a look into one of the sites and can confirm the intel is good. Let me know when the UAVs are on station."

"Will do. What happened to your cooperative Quds soldier?"

"He met the same fate as the rest of his team."

"All of them?"

"No, one of them got away. He was a sniper."

"Expect him to be tracking you."

"Good point."

"Will he know you conducted an interrogation on one of his team?"

"He'll know they're missing a body and probably draw that conclusion."

"They might try to move the missiles. They'll definitely be on high alert."

"They have no way of knowing what my purpose is in Yemen, but I agree they'll take steps to safeguard all ongoing operations since they know we nabbed one of their own."

"We haven't handed Colonel Shalmani over to the Omanis yet. We don't want the Iranians to know we have him until this operation is finished."

"I need to move now."

"Roger, out."

Chapter 16

Sana'a, Yemen

The trip through Sana'a was necessitated by time constraints. Bypassing it would have taken hours Pat didn't have. The sun was low in the winter sky by the time he entered the congested city. Sana'a lies in a bowl, surrounded by high mountains on all sides. He had been riding his motorcycle offroad for the past two hours through some of the scariest terrain he had ever dared on a bike. It was a relief to finally be on flat level ground. Despite the growing shadows, he kept the dark sun visor over his face. With the bandana over the lower part of his face, he was inconspicuous as a Westerner.

He avoided the roads and instead used the narrow side streets and alleyways. The city was a dense concentration of two- and three-story buildings in red brick and white stone. Not a single road was straight; it was a labyrinth of congestion. Large swaths of the city had been leveled by Saudi bombings, entire city blocks reduced to rubble. Gaunt, hollow-eyed people could be seen walking the streets. Sana'a had an air of despair.

Pat spotted a man selling fuel from a partially filled five-gallon water bottle on the side of the road. He pulled over and gave the man five thousand Yemeni rial, the equivalent of twenty dollars, to fill the Kawasaki's fuel tank.

The moon had risen by the time he exited the city and continued off-road toward the mountains in the southeast. He rode for an hour and halted when the GPS mounted on his bike showed he was at the dismount point, one mile from his objective. The hills had been growing steeper and more treacherous, and he was grateful to have only dumped the bike once. Night vision goggles are terrible for depth perception, and he was amazed the bike was still working after hitting so many ditches and rocks.

After hiding the bike, Pat hiked southeast, uphill toward the rocky foothills, taking an angle that would intersect with the only road that led into the mountains for many miles. The road had been built to service a limestone quarry, and if the section he was on was any indication, it was more than adequate for use by a missile carrier. The sky was cloudless, and the moon was nearly full. The green images of intensified light passing through his night vision goggles were crisp and clear.

He held his Glock 19 in his right hand. He would have preferred to keep it in the holster, but when he added the combination laser light and a suppressor, it no longer fit in his holster. The terrain began to close, forming a canyon, forcing him to walk on the road instead of parallel to it.

"Houston, this is Eagle," he heard over the earpiece stuck in his left ear. He reached under his jacket and turned up the volume on the Harris Falcon III radio attached to his plate carrier and then moved his hand to his collar and depressed the PTT switch.

"Eagle, this is Houston," Pat said.

"Be alert, you have a guard five hundred meters further up the road. He's sitting on the north side, behind a barrier, next to a guard shack. Over." Pat imagined a CIA ops officer drinking coffee in the CAOC in Doha, talking to him through a series of UAV relays.

136

"Roger, Eagle. Any other activity in the vicinity? Over," he replied.

"Negative, just the one."

"Roger, out."

Pat slowed his pace and walked as stealthily as possible as he approached the guard. After several minutes of walking, he saw the bright green glow of a cigarette further up the road. Trapped within the walls of the canyon, he continued to advance.

The canyon walls shadowed the light from the moon, making it more difficult to see. As he moved closer, he made out the form of a man sitting behind a wooden pike that could be raised or lowered to allow vehicles to enter and exit. The man had a rifle next to him, propped up against his chair. There was a guard shack nearby, but it appeared empty.

Pat continued his slow advance. When he got within fifty meters, he could see the man's eyes. The guard appeared to be looking straight at him; still, he showed no signs of having detected Pat. He inched forward, making sure to keep to the middle of the road. If the man did see him and opened fire, he didn't want to get hit by the ricochets off the canyon wall.

He advanced cautiously, holding the pistol in front with both hands, his fingers on the trigger and his thumb on the laser select. When he reached within thirty meters, the man jolted upright in his seat and his arm dropped to reach for the weapon.

Pat placed the IR laser on the man's chest and fired two suppressed 9mm rounds in quick succession. He raced to the man as he was still falling backward in his chair and finished him with a shot to the head.

Hiding the body inside the guard shack, Pat continued on his way up the road. Beyond the guard shack, the canyon opened up and revealed a closed limestone mining operation. He reached a fork, with one dirt road spiraling downward into an open quarry mine and the second continuing upward toward the hills. The Quds prisoner had told him all of the missiles were stored in caves, which the big open-pit mine was decidedly not. Pat took the left fork to the high ground.

The road ended at the entrance to another mine—only this one went into the hillside. Originally expecting a cave, Pat was surprised to discover the clean, straight beams of a mine entryway. He stopped and studied the entryway that was fifty meters in front of him, then slowly turned, making a full circle as he scanned the surrounding area. Finding no signs of security, he slowly advanced toward the mine entry.

The first sign of trouble was the staccato blast of automatic gunfire. Pat hit the ground after a volley of tracers flew over his head and frantically crawled toward the mine entrance, which was the closest cover. Green tracer bullets whizzed all around him. When the ground next to him was raked with fire, he sprung upright and sprinted to the entryway. Ten feet from the protection of the mine, a sledgehammer-like force slammed into his back and shoulders, knocking him facefirst to the ground. He scrambled the remaining distance to the mine and hid behind one of the thick wooden beams framing the sides of the entryway.

He couldn't move his left arm. With the pistol in his right hand, he flipped on the infrared flashlight attached to the bottom of his pistol barrel. With the IR flashlight and his night vision goggles, he could see the mine was deep. He caught a reflection of a truck windshield one hundred to perhaps one hundred and fifty meters in. The firing had stopped, but his pulse still pounded, and he could feel blood seeping down his back. He heard voices yelling to each other in Persian and sensed the enemy was closing in for the kill. He rose to his feet unsteadily and moved deeper into the cave, toward the truck.

He assumed the Iranians would be cautious firing into the mine. Careless fire could destroy the missile system they were assigned to protect. He wove his way to the truck and turned on his flashlight again to inspect the cargo. When he saw the big box of a cruise missile launcher mounted on the bed of the truck, he knew he had found his target. The seal was intact, which meant the weapon was armed with a missile.

Pat needed to send a message to Eagle. He tried to reach the CAOC with his radio, but he was too deep inside the mine for the signal to get out. He hugged the side of the mine walls until he got back to the entryway behind the wooden beam. Turning on his IR aiming laser, he scanned the exterior, slowly revealing himself in a pie maneuver. He spotted two Iranian commandos advancing with weapons ready. Because they were wearing body armor, he put the IR laser at face height and quick-fired three rounds at each. Both men went down, but given his present condition, he wasn't sure he'd hit them. Rounds began ricocheting off the beam and entryway to the cave from an enemy position he still couldn't see.

With his one good hand, he reloaded his pistol with a fresh fifteen-round magazine, even though he still had five rounds left in the old mag. Another burst of gunfire hit near him. As soon as the shooter stopped to reload, Pat jumped to the other side of the doorway. When the rifle fire returned against his old location, Pat could see a lone assaulter only twenty-five meters from the entryway, advancing toward the mine. Another Iranian provided cover fire for the assaulter. Pat shot the exposed gunman and emptied half of his magazine in the direction of the soldier providing cover fire as he ran out of the mine.

Fully exposed in the open, Pat knew it was only a matter of seconds before the gunner reacquired him. He saw a mound he could use for cover and slid behind it as tracer gunfire once again pursued him. Hiding behind a pile of sand the size of a car, Pat had his back to the enemy, who he assumed was slowly moving to a vantage point where he could engage him. Pat had better visibility with his night vision, but the Quds soldier had superior range because of his rifle.

Taking advantage of the lull, he placed the pistol on his lap and triggered the PTT switch of his radio with his good hand. Blood seeped down his torso, and he was having difficulty breathing.

"Eagle, this is Houston," he said in a raspy voice.

"Eagle over."

"Intel is good. I can confirm one missile at site number four."

"Roger."

"I need close air now. Where's that Reaper? Don't you have a visual on the tango that's stalking me?"

"Reaper can't engage. It's been danger close since the beginning. Your target is walking toward the hill you're hiding behind."

"Let me know what he does when he gets here. Any updates on my JTAC teams?"

"JTAC is airborne. TOT is in forty-five mikes."

"Roger."

"Tango is directly opposite you on the little hill. He's moving clockwise, very slowly."

Pat took his one good hand off the PTT and recovered his pistol, aiming it to his left, where he expected the enemy soldier to emerge. He laid his head back and rested his helmet against the sand, bringing his left leg in toward his chest so he could rest the weakened hand holding the pistol on his knee. He slowed his breath.

After what seemed like an eternity, the barrel of a rifle poked around the corner of the sandpile. Unable to see behind the sandpile, the gunner sensed his presence and fired blindly behind the hill without exposing himself. The rounds barely missed Pat, who maintained his focus through his night vision. After using up most of his magazine with the first automatic burst, the gunner rushed around the corner and fired a second burst. Before he could lower his weapon onto his target, Pat shot him twice in the face with his pistol.

Pat struggled to his knees. Using both hands to push himself up, he stood erect and leaned against the sandpile. His earbud was making noise, but it was unintelligible through the dizziness. He began to weave and stagger down the road. The downhill slope made it easier to cover ground. He knew he had to get out of the area because a thirty-thousand-pound bomb was going to be dropped on the hill very soon. He pushed himself as hard as he could as his breathing became increasingly labored. Eventually, his vision narrowed, and he staggered and fell. He tried to get up several times, but after the third attempt, everything went black.

Chapter 17

McDonald, Migos, Burnia and Jankowski sat on the mesh nylon cargo seats in the cargo compartment of the C130. The plane lifted off from UAE's Al Dhafra Air Force Base and began the ninety-minute flight to the jump area over Yemen. The men wore RAM-1 parachutes, helmets with night vision goggles attached, body armor and navaids connected to their chests. Between each man's legs was a multicam rucksack containing a PRC-117 radio and an EJTAC-LTD laser target designator.

Twenty minutes before the drop, the men were conducting equipment checks. The only light in the cabin was a red light. The cabin noise was loud, but the ramp door had not yet been opened and it was still possible to talk. Bill Sachse, the load master, approached the men. He was wearing a headset.

"UAVs report that all observation points are clear. We have confirmation the intel was good and the missiles are in the target areas."

The men signaled they understood with a thumbs-up.

"Jankowski, Pat's moving to link up with you at your observation point. He's been wounded."

"How bad?" Jankowski asked.

"Unknown. This is all being relayed from the CAOC over the SATCOM. TOT for the first B-2 is 0200. Extraction has been moved up to 0230, or immediately after the strike."

The ramp dropped and in sequence, Sachse gave the signal for each jumper to drop based on his respective target location. It was a HAHO jump. The men jumped at ten thousand feet and deployed their parachutes at five thousand to achieve the most precise navigation possible.

Jankowski expertly landed on the small hilltop overlooking site four. He released his chute and bundled it up, then stuffed it inside the parachute bag he carried. He confirmed his location with his GPS and oriented himself to the terrain. The visibility was excellent with the full moon, and using his NVGs, he could see an open-pit mine below him and, five hundred meters beyond, the hole in the mountain where the cruise missile was stored.

He retrieved the LTD and powered it up. The system weighed only five pounds. For accuracy he set it up on a small tripod. On the Picatinny rail located on top of the LTD, he mounted a BAE UTC Xii thermal optic. Sitting on the rocky ridge with the tripod between his legs, he surveyed the target, starting with the cave opening. At a range of two thousand meters, he could see that the cave was actually a mine entry. He found a body lying in the entryway. Scanning around the mine entrance, he found three more. He followed the road running from the mine all the way to the guard shack.

Beyond the guard shack, the road was masked by the walls of a canyon. He followed the ridgeline on the top of the canyon until it opened up again and he could see the road. He spotted a body lying off the side of the road and, triggering the laser range finder, he learned the body was 1,572 meters from his location and he estimated about another nine hundred meters from the cave entrance. Because of the distance involved, he couldn't be sure the body was Pat, but he had a strong suspicion.

Over his headset, Jankowski heard "Trident one, this is Misty FAC."

He heard Migos's voice reply, "Misty, this is Trident one."

"Confirm your location with IR strobe."

"Misty, strobe on."

"Roger, location confirmed."

"Trident one, mark tango one in ten seconds."

"Misty, laser on 1688"

"Spot, cease laser, set 1688."

"Trident one, are we clear to engage? Over."

"Affirmative, clear to engage."

"Aircraft moving to the IP. Stand by to lase for ninety seconds on my order."

"Wilco, out."

Misty went through the same sequence for Burnia and McDonald. The sequence repeated until the question came about the blast area.

"Trident four, are we clear to engage?"

"Misty, negative. I have a suspected friendly less than a kilometer from the target. Over."

"Trident, spot the target with your laser pointer in ten."

"Misty, laser on."

"Spot, cease laser. I confirm, that's a friendly. Location was already provided from earlier intel."

"Is he danger close?"

"Affirmative, danger close. Engagement is cleared from higher. Stand by to lase on my order. Maintain lase for ninety seconds. Aircraft are moving to the IP. Separation on TOT is two minutes."

"Roger, out."

The four sites were all within ten kilometers of one another. Jankowski heard and felt the first three air strikes. Crouched behind the EJTAC, his back was beginning to stiffen. He oriented the thermal at Pat one more time before returning to his target at the crest of the hill five hundred feet above the mine entrance. Pat still had not moved.

"Trident four, this is Misty. Ten seconds."

"Misty, this is Trident four."

"Trident four, laser on."

Jankowski triggered the laser target designator and waited. He tried to imagine what was going on in the sky above him. At ten thousand feet, the Reapers were loitering, supplying the analysts back in Doha and Langley with the imagery needed to make a battle damage assessment. At fifteen thousand feet was Misty, the forward air controller, orbiting in a slow-moving OA-10 Thunderbolt. At twenty-two thousand feet was a huge wing-shaped B-2 bomber releasing a massive thirty-thousand-pound GBU-57 with a Paveway II guidance kit though its bomb bay doors.

Jankowski maintained pressure on the trigger as he looked through the thermal sight mounted on top of his EJTAC. The communication between Misty and Broadsword, the B-2 bomber, was done on a different frequency. Jankowski's radio net was silent; he was left with nothing but the thought of how close Pat was to the target.

At the top of the screen of his thermals, he thought he detected an impact on the top of the hill. Still, he maintained pressure on the laser designator, just in case he was mistaken. Seconds later, a huge flame erupted from the mine entryway, follow by a blast that sent rocks and debris everywhere as the entire hill erupted in an explosion. A dust cloud engulfed the impact area, and it soon became impossible to see either the hill or the cave. He shifted the thermal viewer to Pat, but even that far from the blast, the dust cloud obscured his vision.

Jankowski packed up his rucksack with the radio and the EJTAC, grabbed his M4A1 carbine, and with the speed of a gifted athlete, he bounded down from his perch toward Pat's location.

"Misty, this Trident four."

"Trident four, this is Misty."

"I'm moving to the man down. Request cover."

"I've got a full magazine and we have two Reapers on station with Hellfire. I have you covered."

It took fifteen minutes for Jankowski to reach Pat. As he approached, he heard the rotor blades of the extraction MH-60. By the time the helicopter landed on the road behind him, he had cut off Pat's jacket and vest, sealed the wound in his back where the round had slipped behind his body armor and entered his lung, plugged the hole in his shoulder with Celox and started an IV. He was unrolling a pole-less litter when Migos, Burnia and McDonald arrived from the MH-60, and the four of them carried Pat up the embankment to the road and the waiting chopper.

McDonald the medic took over the treatment inside the helicopter. The next stop was an aircraft carrier, the USS *Gerald Ford*, on patrol in the Sea of Aden.

Pat was rushed into surgery. Twelve hours later, he was evacuated to the US Army Regional Hospital in Landstuhl, Germany. Two weeks later, Pat was in the Bahamas.

Chapter 18

Eleuthera, Bahamas

Pat relaxed his body as he tumbled through the water. The salt stung his eyes as his body reached neutral buoyancy. He became oriented when he was able to see the brightness that represented the way up. Reinforcing the path to oxygen, the leash attached to his ankle began to tug him upward into the frothy surf. He finally broke through to the surface and retrieved his board. He held the board under him with both hands and rode the white surf lying flat on his chest until the water became shallow enough to stand, and then he walked the remaining stretch to the shore.

When he reached the pink sand of the beach, he found his old friend Mike Guthrie standing at the water's edge.

"You stayed down a long time. Surprising endurance for a one-lunged wonder," Mike said.

"It was just a little puncture. I still have two good airbags," replied Pat.

"You've healed up pretty well if you can surf in these conditions," Mike said.

"Yeah, I feel good. It's great physical therapy, especially for the shoulder."

The two men walked side by side toward Pat's beach house. When they arrived, they climbed the exterior stairs to the second-story deck and sat down. Mike wore beige Bermuda shorts and a gray USMA sweatshirt. Pat was sporting a 3mm black-and-aqua Tyr wet suit.

Maria, the young Filipina who managed the house, opened the sliding glass door and handed Pat a towel. She returned a few minutes later with a coffee setting.

"Maria looks after you pretty well," Mike said.

"She does. She and Jonah, her husband, just had a second baby, but somehow she still manages to keep everything in the house running smoothly. She's about the only woman I seem to be able to keep in my life," Pat said.

"I'm sure it's been rough," Mike said.

"I won't lie, it has. These last few days have been the worst."

"It'll get better with time," Mike said.

"I'm not so sure. I had to leave Abu Dhabi in a hurry and I had a bunch of food in my boat that was going to go bad. So, I'm in the hospital in Germany and I call Migos. I'm half whacked on morphine, and I wind up offering him the use of my boat in exchange for cleaning it up. Now, I can track the boat by remotely accessing the navigation system on the damn thing. He's had it docked in Dubai for the past three days. Can you imagine what he's doing to my boat?"

"Migos." Mike chuckled. "I'm sure he brought help."

"Stupidest decision of my life. This is why people shouldn't take drugs. You know they're drinking my premium wine stash, and I can't even imagine what's happening in my cabin."

"He wouldn't use the owner's cabin."

"You don't know Migos. He has a thing for those Eastern European supermodel types. The uber gold diggers who move to Dubai to strike it rich. He couldn't sell the yacht as his own unless he was using the owner's cabin. I guarantee you he's defiling my sanctuary with someone named Svetlana as we speak."

"We should call him," Mike said, laughing.

"I've tried. He's not picking up."

"You should buy a new boat. You can afford it."

"You'd think so, but I really can't. Remember all those bitcoins I told you about last year?"

"Yes, you had about twenty million."

"Well, that became a whole hell of a lot more. I sold at the peak of the tulip frenzy. I was flush, and I was looking at some incredible yachts."

"What happened?"

"Father Tellez happened. One minute, I'm feeling sorry for myself, seeking consolation in the world's greatest man toy. The next thing you know, he launches into the 'children are starving in Venezuela' speech and guilts me out of it."

"You gave your bitcoin windfall to the foundation?"

"Starving kids versus a Jacuzzi on the top deck—it was a brutal decision. The padre has a way of getting what he wants. He might actually be playing for the other team. You should run a background on him."

"I had breakfast with him this morning. He's definitely the real thing."

"As a consolation, I'm going to do a complete overhaul on the *Sam Houston*."

"Are you interested in the operations summary?"

"Yeah, of course."

"BDA was definitive. All three cruise missile systems were destroyed. Sultan Asaad is one grateful American-loving Omani monarch. The crown prince of UAE also gave us his thanks. He's now an even bigger fan of Pat Walsh. You may want to ask him for a new boat."

"What I would really like to ask him is whose idea it was to put two nuclear reactors in the middle of most volatile land in the planet. He owns about ten percent of the world's oil—you'd think he has enough oil and gas to keep the lights on."

"I wouldn't recommend that."

"I've been reading the papers. Seems the Hezbollah mother of all rocket attacks was underwhelming."

"Israel is under different management than in 2006. This guy didn't make selective strikes and follow with a ground attack to minimize collateral damage. He swatted the first two waves of rockets down with Iron Dome, and before they could fully reload, he leveled entire city blocks with thousands of his own rockets."

"That's the first time in a while Iran has had to put one up on the loss column."

"They put three losses up. They failed to destabilize Oman, they failed with Israel, and they failed to take out the UAE's nuclear power plants."

"Your CIA bosses must be happy campers," Pat said.

"The president called me himself. They watched the UAV feed on your mission from the situation room."

"With all those eyes in the sky and all the observers, why didn't somebody warn me before I got shot?"

"Did you see who shot you?"

"No. I remember scanning the area and then turning my back and moving toward the mine entrance. The next thing I know, everything just went to hell."

"We had a Reaper on station, the same one that identified and warned you about the first guard. The UAV didn't spot who shot you either. We're talking about a full sensor package—DMTI, SAR, IR, the works. The four guys who engaged you came out of nowhere. They were completely masked."

"How is that possible?"

"They must have been inside a blind with advanced overhead cover to block any sensors from the UAV. It must have also had camouflage on the sides to block your night vision. Overhead surveillance is so prevalent these days, the bad guys are getting very skilled at defeating it."

"The Iranians are getting sophisticated. That's a very painful lesson learned."

"I kept up on your condition. I'm sure it was."

"How long are you in town?" Pat asked.

"I fly back to Langley tomorrow."

"We can go to Tippy's for dinner. Drink some beer, maybe hook up with tourists," Pat said.

"I'm married."

"You can be my wingman. Just tell the ladies that I'm a secret agent, and be sure to mention that the president watches me from the White House Situation Room while I save the world from Dr. Evil."

"That will never happen."

"Sometimes, you disappoint me, Mike. What's next on the agenda? My team has probably burned through half of their last bonus check and are looking for something to do, beyond drunkenness, debauchery and destroying my boat."

"That's the reason I'm here. Why don't you change out of that wet suit and we can talk after you shower? Best to talk upstairs in your office."

The office was on the third floor of the house and had huge picture windows facing both east and west. The view to the east was of the Atlantic Ocean, where Pat had been surfing earlier. The water was a dark green, and the shoreline was white with foam from the breaking swells. Closer in, the pink beach sand for which Eleuthera was famous could be seen through the palm trees. Further out, the two guest houses came into view with an infinity swimming pool located between them. To the west, the calmer turquoise waters of the Caribbean dominated the scene. At its widest, the one-hundred-mile-long Eleuthera Island was less than a mile wide, which was what made it possible for Pat's beach home to straddle two such magnificent bodies of water.

The two men sat opposite each other in leather easy chairs with a coffee table between, upon which sat two plates loaded with sandwiches. Maria deposited the food and drinks and silently exited the room by the elevator.

"What do you want us to do?" Pat asked Mike.

"This next task isn't a single mission. It's more of a campaign. Most likely it'll take months, maybe even years. It's going to take me a little time to explain."

"Okay."

"Mind if I finish lunch first?"

"Not at all. Maria's a good cook. Who ever heard of a Filipina who could make a Cuban sandwich?"

"It must be the Caribbean influence."

"She's gifted."

After they finished, Pat made coffee.

"Up until fifteen years ago, Hezbollah was strictly a terrorist organization. The Quds funded a group of Lebanese Shia imams after the Iranian revolution in 1979 and then pointed them at Israel and the United States. Their first big victory was the Beirut bombing that blew up two hundred and twenty Marines in eighty-three. Back in the eighties, Hezbollah was shunned by the civilized world and supported only by Iran." Mike sipped his coffee.

"Today they're still a terrorist organization, but they've branched out. They have a conventional military that's more of a militia force, which they deployed to Syria in big numbers. They're the dominant political party in Lebanon. They control the Lebanese government. They're also one of the world's most successful organized crime syndicates."

"Organized crime, really?" Pat asked.

"Hezbollah's sales of cocaine and weapons that were imported into the US and Mexico last year exceeded two billion dollars. They're also active in Western Europe," Mike said.

"How did that happen?"

"Historically, Hezbollah's major source of income has been Iran. The sanctions against Iran eventually became so severe that the money flowing into Hezbollah was reduced to a trickle. Necessity being the mother of invention, they eventually discovered creative ways to supplement that income."

"Arabs aren't well known for organized crime. They're not known for organized anything, if we were to be honest."

"The DEA's progress against the cartels in Mexico and Colombia gave Hezbollah the opening they needed," Mike said. "The problem was big enough to become a top priority by 2006. A joint task force consisting of DOJ, FBI, DEA and CIA was created to tackle it."

"But," Pat said.

"But, in 2008 we got a new administration who felt we needed to build bridges with the Iranians. The priority shifted to pursuing a deal to shut down Iran's progress toward a nuclear weapon. It was felt the joint task force would jeopardize the warming relations between the two countries, so the JTF was mothballed," Mike said.

"Now what?"

"Without any serious law enforcement efforts to curtail their activities, the money is flooding into Hezbollah. The Iranians are flush because they can sell oil again, and hundreds of billions of dollars of their assets were unfrozen as part of the nuclear deal. The drug and other criminal operations have gone unchecked for almost a decade, and they've grown enormously."

"You want Trident to concentrate on Hezbollah?" Pat asked.

"Exactly. While the US spins up the capability to address the issue from a law enforcement perspective, we want you to attack it from an extrajudicial perspective."

"Extrajudicial. It's not like you to use terms like that."

"It's not something we ever want to get out in a congressional oversight committee. After sleeping for nearly a decade, the big boys want immediate results."

"Why the urgency?"

"Hezbollah is using the funds they're receiving to corrupt an already corrupt Lebanese political system and take absolute control of the country. They're also using the money to field and deploy military forces in Syria, Yemen and Iraq. The administration intends to slow the funding Hezbollah gets from Iran by eventually reimposing economic sanctions on Iran. But that won't do any good unless we can also curtail the gains they receive from the criminal side of their organization."

"Why Trident?"

"You're the most effective direct-action asset we have in the region."

"Do you have the first target picked out? Do I need to hustle back?"

"Yes, you do."

"Good. I need to salvage the last of the dignity and virtue remaining in the *Sam Houston*. As a Texan, I'm sure you can appreciate that."

"I can."

"You just know Migos and those gold diggers are breaking into the good stuff. I guarantee, they won't stop with the Pappy Van Winkle and the bourbon collection. They'll find their way into the single malts, and I shudder to think what they'll do to the cognacs. My Napoleon is finished, I promise you."

"Believe it or not, that is not a typical complaint I hear from our people in the field."

"I hear you, but I'm having visions of Migos coupling with some Estonian model on my damn Italian leather. He's got that whole Muy Muy Migos line, where he is just so much more."

"I've always wondered why a Greek American describes himself with Spanish adjectives."

"He didn't give himself the name. An Hispanic NCO in his unit gave it to him as a putdown, because he was so full of himself. In typical Migos form, he thought it was a compliment. He liked it, so he took it as his own."

"He's a colorful character. You need to head back to UAE ASAP."

"Definitely. Send whatever you have by way of a target list to David Forrest. We'll work the planning out of Paphos. Most likely we'll launch from UAE."

"The first mission is in Dubai, the money-laundering capital of the world and a hub for Hezbollah banking and finance. Many of the bad guys are operating out of Dubai, which is another reason you're the best choice for this operation. You have a lot of goodwill with the leadership."

"I'm convinced. Operation Save My Yacht from Migos is officially launched and underway."

Later in the evening, the two men sat at a table at Tippy's restaurant, which was a short walk from the house. It was early evening, and the open-air restaurant was packed with tourists. The band was between sets, and the only noise beyond the din of conversation from the crowd and the pounding surf from the beach.

"How is the conch soup?" Pat asked.

"Excellent," replied Mike.

"You know if they called it ginormous snail soup, nobody would order it."

"Very funny," Mike said.

"Just an observation."

The band was setting up. The keyboardist, drummer, lead guitarist and bass player were already on stage, going through whatever rituals bands engage in before playing. The lead singer was a bottle blonde with pretensions. As a regular, Pat had been watching her and was not impressed with her work ethic. She never helped with the setup, and she was always the last on stage. She liked to make an entrance befitting her future celebrity.

"Do you want to talk about Susu?" Mike asked.

"I think we should focus on food and rum drinks that are served with umbrellas," Pat said, tipping his drink.

"That's it?"

The two men sat in silence for several minutes. Both pretended to be distracted by the aspiring diva's entrance. Finally, Pat broke the silence.

"I was robbed, and I'm pissed, but what can I do? There was no good reason for them to kill Susu or anyone else in that hotel. When we captured Colonel Shalmani, I was tempted to just beat the life out of him, but I didn't. It wasn't going to make me feel any better. The man's a reptile. In the end, he did what he was trained and conditioned to do. I blame the people he works for."

Mike nodded, signaling Pat to go on.

"This latest initiative you have is a good start. But it's not going to solve the problem. The Quds Force is not a young organization. They've been cranking out psycho fanatics like Shalmani since seventy-nine. These nutjobs got their start giving twelve-year-old kids wooden keys to heaven during the Iran-Iraq war in 1980. They used to order children to charge into minefields covered by machine guns with the promise that they were going to paradise. Over a million were killed in that war. How can we seriously believe that we're going to make an impact on people capable of such things by taking out the minions involved in money laundering and drug running?"

"What are you getting at?"

"We need to go after the big fish. I want to kill the commander of the Iranian Revolutionary Guard, the guy who created Shalmani and the people like him. Then I want to kill his successor and his successor's successor. They manage Hezbollah, and I think the best way to accomplish the mission you gave me earlier is to decapitate the organization," Pat said.

"That's insane. You're talking about conducting major combat operations in Tehran," Mike said.

"What's the downside? The Iranians discover we don't like them?"

"The downside is you die."

"Let me look into the possibility. If the opportunity presents itself, all I ask is you give me a hearing and then a green light if it looks like I can take that guy out."

"Is that going to help you grieve for Susu?"

"It's the payback Susu deserves. Torching the Chedi was the evilest act I've ever seen. I've seen a lot and I'm no saint myself. The Iranians are training. They're growing and cultivating people who commit atrocities like that, and the biggest reason why is because of Commander Wooden Key. He needs to go. Period."

"I don't disagree with you. We keep tabs on the guy. He used to be a field operator, even as a general. He was wounded three years ago in Syria, and ever since then, he doesn't leave Iran. Going after him in Tehran is suicidal. Believe me, you're not the first to consider it."

"I can do it."

"Pat, you're my friend. You're my best friend. I've known you for over thirty years. I have a section within the Middle East section that has no purpose other than to support you. I know the people who you care about, like Migos."

"How does that matter?"

"The Pat Walsh I know would have raged when Susu died. He would have beaten Colonel Shalmani to a bloody pulp."

"Maybe I'm evolving."

"I'm worried you may have given up. Going after the Quds commander is looking for a way to die. There are people who work for me. People whose only job is to study every psych eval you've ever taken, whose job is to study and predict your behavior, who think you're looking for a way to end it."

"Because of Susu."

"It's cumulative. You've had some tough breaks. But, yeah, Susu is the last straw."

They were interrupted by a heavyset middle-aged Bahamian woman who brought the main courses. Pat had grouper and Mike had crab and shrimp linguini. The two men attacked their respective dinners while the Miley Cyrus lookalike launched into Rihanna's "Man Down."

"The world is definitely a lot less interesting and fun without Susu in it. But any idea that I'm looking for a dignified exit is wrong. The mission in Yemen was high-risk. Doing the job with two men would have been riskier than going in alone, and I was the best person on my team for that specific task, so I did it myself."

"I agree with you on that point. I don't think anyone else would have pulled it off."

"I think you would also agree that the mission needed to be done. Let's face it, if those cruise missiles had slammed into the UAE's nuclear reactors, it would have been a very bad thing."

"I agree with you on that point as well."

"Then why all the naval-gazing Dr. Phil bullshit about my motives?"

"Before I came here, I briefed the director. The task he wanted you to perform was to roll up the criminal money-making enterprises of Hezbollah. If I come back to him with a plan to off the commanding general of the Quds Force, he's going to question my sanity."

"And my sanity."

"Your sanity has been in question for a long time."

"When have I ever failed to accomplish a mission? You want Hezbollah out of the guns and drugs business. We both know they're working for Quds. I'll take out the Quds commander, then, during the rudderless transition period, we can roll up the Lebanese minions."

"Let me take it back. Don't do anything in Iran unless I give you the go-ahead. What you're talking about will require an official finding signed by the president, which is a long shot at best. For the time being, stick to the plan. Don't go rogue on this—it'll become a major problem."

"I have a flight to Dubai tomorrow. I'm going to detox Migos and my boys, send their fallen women to the nunnery, cleanse and possibly conduct an exorcism on my boat, and begin thumping the Iranian and Lebanese money launderers in Dubai as ordered. Is that okay?"

"That's perfect. What are you going to tell Sheikh Mohammed?"

"Do you want me to talk to him? I thought you would do it," Pat said.

"No. Set up a meeting and let him know what you're up to."

"Can you arrange the meeting, and I'll brief him? If the meeting's arranged through official channels, he'll know I'm working with the consent and support of Uncle Sam."

"He'd know that anyway. Stopping those cruise missiles avoided a disaster."

"I'm glad you told him I had a hand in that."

"Yes, I told him myself."

"That's good, because whatever happens in Dubai is likely going to require some UAE governmental support."

"What are you planning on doing in Dubai?" Mike asked.

"Financial stuff. You wouldn't understand it."

"Try me."

"No, you're hopeless. I give you tip after tip, and you never do anything with them."

"I missed out on bitcoin, that's for sure."

"Bitcoin's a bad example," Pat said. "That was just luck, and I was kind of wrong about the euro crashing. Lately, I'm killing it with oil. War is coming to the Middle East, and the risk premium on oil prices is why it's sixty dollars a barrel and heading higher."

The buxom Bahamian waitress replenished their drinks without being asked. It had been a while since Pat had felt so content. He enjoyed his time with Mike. He drew comfort from their conversations and banter. As soon as the waitress left, Mike jumped in.

"You're making money betting that I'll fail at my job?"

"I never really thought of it that way, but yeah, I guess I am."

"Are you really that pessimistic?"

"Not totally. I believe the specter of war actually makes things safer."

"How do you figure?"

"Without the Shia or Iranian threat, the Saudis would've already ditched the US for China. At the moment, only fifteen percent of Saudi oil goes to China. The Saudis refuse to break the agreement they made with Nixon in seventy-four to sell oil in dollars in exchange for US protection. If the Saudis ever abandon the petrodollar, the US economy is going to be in serious trouble."

"Saudis keep the petrodollar agreement because they know the US will defend them, something the Chinese may not do," Mike said.

"Exactly. The moment that protection loses its value is the moment they jump ship for the yuan and the dollar become the peso."

"You have an interesting way of looking at things."

"Nobody got crushed worse than me during the last recession, so you'll never hear me pretending to be clairvoyant." Pat laughed.

"Yeah, but you've made an incredible amount of money."

"I have, but I made most of it in the same way you came out ahead in Oman."

"How's that?" Mike said.

"Luck. If we're being honest, we—you, me and the CIA—screwed up pretty bad. We didn't anticipate the threat from Iran. We didn't anticipate the threat of Hezbollah. We made a lot of incorrect assumptions, but when it was all said and done and the smoke cleared, it all worked out."

"I'm not following you."

"We got lucky. We're just screwing up in the right direction."

"You think so?"

"I do, and I also think it's better to be lucky than good. Please talk to the leadership about letting me take out the Quds commander."

"I will, but I want you to promise that you're not just looking for a way to commit suicide by Quds."

"You have my word, Mike. I have no desire to die. God doesn't want me, and the Devil is afraid I'll take over."

"God wants you. You have Father Tellez in your corner. You pay him all those indulgences, as they're called. Your bitcoin windfall must have been serious money."

"That's not how that works. The theology is misunderstood, and the Trident Foundation was never motivated by that. The foundation is just a charity. Once I made enough money to take care of my family, I wanted to do something worthwhile with it, and I couldn't think of anyone better than Father Tellez to know what that would be. Feeding the starving victims of Bernie Sanders' and Cesar Chavez's kooky religion isn't a bad thing to do, is it?"

"Indulgences don't get you off the fast train to hell."

"No, but they do shorten your stay in purgatory."

"That's something."

"Yeah, if you believe that, which I most certainly do not. Besides, after the pain I've felt after losing Susu, what more could any vengeful deity do to me?"

"I hear you. Back to your plan. Don't get your hopes up. Major General Suleimani is a political target, and taking him out is a political assassination, which is a very sensitive matter. It's likely the big bosses won't approve it."

"Quds just slaughtered dozens of Americans in the Chedi Hotel. They killed hundreds of American soldiers in Iraq with advanced IEDs and wounded thousands more. They just tried to irradiate the Gulf States, which would have spiked oil prices and crashed the American economy. You think the politicos are going flinch at a chance to kill the man responsible?"

"They might flinch, or they might give us the green light. I'm just trying to prepare you in case they say no."

"They'll agree, because Trident gives them deniability. They'll take credit for a success and pretend I never existed if I fail."

"I'll go back and sell the idea of taking out the Quds commander. You go to UAE and begin the planning and preparation for the fight against the organized crime branch of Hezbollah."

Chapter 19

Dubai

The Emirates Airline flight from Miami to Dubai was scheduled to take fourteen and a half hours. Emirates Airbus 380 First Class was an experience unimaginable to most American domestic travelers. On the other hand, the flight from North Eleuthera to Miami was on the other end of the spectrum and sadly not unimaginable to most American domestic travelers. On reflection, Pat considered that this most recent trip might have reached a new low in his long and painful history of riding the cattle cars of domestic submission.

Because it was a last-minute booking, he found himself in the second-to-last row of a tiny MD-90 airplane, his body awkwardly contorted to conform his six-foot-five frame into the window seat with the curved side, which forced him to sit with his upper body angled away from the window. Behind him, a pleasant-looking middle-aged woman and her husband brought their dog along on a leash. The Jack Russell terrier howled for twenty minutes after takeoff and another full twenty minutes on the descent, leaving precious little peace on the hour-long flight. The brief respite from barking was punctuated with the distressed animal relieving itself in the aisle. The elderly woman seated next to Pat, closest to the aisle, became so exasperated at the spectacle that she spent the remainder of the flight quietly sobbing with her face in her hands.

While lining up to depart, Pat spoke to the owners and mentioned that they had a very cute dog. Proud as new parents, they seemed oblivious to the pain the innocent canine had inflicted on the other passengers. He asked if it was a service dog, and the woman replied that it was. With a self-satisfied expression, the effusive pet owner went on to explain that flying with her dog was allowed because it helped relieve her anxiety.

Pat chuckled at that comment as it reminded him how the dog had nearly caused his neighbor to have a mental breakdown. The experience made him wonder what the bottom would look like as the downward spiral of civility and service continued, and just how miserable the American flying experience would have to become before ticket sales fell off the cliff. Lost in thought, his distraction ended when a smiling stewardess entered his suite to take his wine and dinner order.

The Emirates Airline chauffeur dropped him at the Address Hotel in the Dubai Marina. Once he was settled, he walked out onto the marina walkway in search of his boat. He had been unable to spot it from his room but assumed it was masked by the building.

It was a beautiful weekend winter afternoon. The walkway around the marina was congested with people enjoying the warm sunny weather, shopping, exercising and sightseeing. Unable to spot his yacht, Pat went to the marina office and asked. The person behind the counter told him that it was out and would return later. Pat thanked the man for pointing out the *Sam Houston*'s boat slip and then went back to his room.

As the sun began to set, Pat watched the *Sam Houston* slowly navigate the narrow waterway. Ten to fifteen people were on deck, many still in swimsuits. At the flybridge helm was Roger McDonald, who expertly backed the sixty-four-foot vessel into the narrow slip. Pat left the room and made his way to the boat.

The last time anyone on the team had seen Pat, he was barely conscious on a stretcher that was being loaded aboard a C-2 aircraft on the carrier deck of the *Gerald Ford*.

The music from the yacht's outside speaker system was loud. The party was still going full tilt. McDonald noticed Pat first; he appeared to be the only sober member of the crowd and was supervising the docking procedure.

Migos must have seen Pat through the salon window, because he darted through the salon doors to the stern deck and hopped the side wall to greet him in a crushing bear hug. Jankowski and Burnia were next, and finally McDonald once he finished shutting down the engines and tying everything down.

"Welcome back," they each said in one way or another. Pat noticed the revelers were not disappearing and he figured there was an after-party planned.

"Look, I don't want to hold you up. I'm staying next door at the Address. Meet me at two tomorrow afternoon. Don't leave anything on the boat. It's going in tomorrow morning for an overhaul and refurb," Pat said.

"Come with us. We're going to Pier 7," Migos said as he wrapped his arm around a young lady who looked like she had a future as a Victoria's Secret model.

"No, you guys have fun. I have some things to take care of. Make the most of your night. Tomorrow you go back to work," Pat said.

The cluster of revelers drifted down the marina walkway toward the Pier 7 building less than a quarter mile distant.

McDonald stayed back. A team of cleaners descended on the boat and went to work. Pat and McDonald climbed up to the flybridge.

"We had a lot of downtime. I hope you don't mind our using the boat," said McDonald.

"No, I don't mind. I'm glad you've all had some time to enjoy yourselves," Pat lied.

"What's the next job?"

"I'm going to take this boat to Ajman tomorrow morning and turn it over to Gulf Craft. Tomorrow at the meeting, I'll brief everyone on what lies ahead. It's a long and somewhat complicated discussion. This isn't the best place to have it. This boat hasn't been swept for bugs in ages."

"Yeah, that makes sense," replied the former DEVGRU member.

"It's good to be back. How's everyone doing?" Pat asked.

"Ready to go back to work. Two months of hanging around gets old after a while."

"That's not going to be a problem anymore."

"How are you feeling?"

"I'm a hundred percent. I did a lot of swimming and surfing in the Bahamas. I'm rested and ready, same as the rest of the team."

"You want some help taking the boat over to Ajman tomorrow?"

"Yeah, that would be good. I was going to leave at eight."

"What are your plans tonight?"

"I have dinner with a guy I hope can help with information. I'm looking for intel for the next op. You're welcome to come along if you want."

"It's not too high-level for me?"

"Nothing's too high-level for you. Be warned, the guy's a bit of a bullshitter, but if you can separate the Israeli exaggeration from the truth, he's an encyclopedia of knowledge."

"What's his name?"

"Pinni Cohen. He's an international man of mystery who dabbles in the gun trade and contracts himself out to UAE National Security on technical matters. He claims to be former Mossad, but more than likely he's still active," Pat replied.

"How do you know him?"

"I sometimes use him as a go-between for purchases from Israel. He has a good track record when it comes to getting the Israeli government's approval to export items. He's especially good at bringing intel systems into UAE without raising a lot of red flags."

Dinner that evening with Pini and McDonald was at Zuma, located in the financial district. Pini had arranged for the reservation, which hadn't been easy to get on short notice and was an indicator of how big a player he was in Dubai. When he and McDonald arrived, the hostess took them to a round table in the corner of the dining room. Pini was already seated. With his back to the wall, he was able to survey everything taking place in the dining room.

Pini had once mentioned to Pat that he had been a tank commander during the 1973 war. Pat placed him in his late sixties, although he looked much younger. He was bald, tan and fit, with a compact body and intelligent piercing blue eyes. Originally from Poland, he was an Israeli citizen who traveled with a UK passport.

Pini was a gifted storyteller. The wine flowed, and the courses of Zuma specialties were delivered with perfect timing. McDonald was clearly enjoying himself. Pini was a gossip, and his stories regarding the shenanigans of the local monarchs were hilarious. Finally, after the grilled toothfish and wagyu beef cheek, Pat raised his hands to signal he had reached his limit.

The men were drinking coffee when Pini finally got down to business.

"Thank you for inviting me to dinner. It's been wonderful. But surely you want more from me than my ability to get a dinner reservation."

"I do. I have some questions I was hoping you could answer."

"Please, feel free."

"The difficulty with the questions is they're going to indicate some things to you regarding my future activities. If you were to disclose this conversation to the wrong people, then it could cause me and my people some harm."

"I've always been discreet."

"I know you have, but this is more sensitive than anything we've discussed in the past. I thought it would be helpful to spell out who you can and cannot share this conversation with."

"I'm fine with that, if it gives you comfort."

"It does. You know who I am, and you know who I work for. I'm less clear with you. I want your word that you will not share this conversation with anyone except Mossad. Nobody else, no other government."

"You have my word."

"Excellent. Tell us what you know about Qassem Suleimani."

"That's going to take a lot of time. I know a lot about that man. You may want to order another bottle of wine."

A pretty Asian waitress in a black evening gown was hovering around the table, looking to deliver the check and turn the table over. Pat wasn't sure if she was the same waitress who had been serving them, because the lighting was so dim and they all seemed to be clones of each other. Pat signaled her over.

"I'm sorry to inconvenience you. We'd like another bottle of that same Grand Cru. My friend here has a story to tell, and it looks like we're going to be a while longer." He pressed a thousand-dirham note into the young lady's hand.

Pini had a flair for the dramatic. He waited for the wine to be poured and then began.

"Major General Qassem Suleimani is the commander of the most powerful and elite branch of the Revolutionary Guard, called the Quds Force. The force is the sharpest instrument of Iranian foreign policy. They're the equivalent of the CIA and US Special Forces combined. The name Quds comes from the Persian word for Jerusalem. The liberation of Jerusalem is the reason Quds was created.

"Suleimani was born in Rabor, an impoverished mountain village in eastern Iran. When he was a boy, his father, like many other farmers, took out an agricultural loan from the government of the shah. When the farm faltered, Suleimani was forced to leave home and work as a laborer. As you can imagine, working as a laborer at the age of ten to keep his father from going to debtors' prison left him with a deep resentment toward the shah.

"In 1979, when Suleimani was twenty-two, the shah fell to a popular uprising led by Ayatollah Khomeini. Although not a religious man, he was swept up in the fervor and joined the Revolutionary Guard, a force established by Iran's new clerical leadership to prevent the military from mounting a coup. He advanced rapidly. As a young guardsman, his first action was in northwestern Iran, where he helped crush an uprising by ethnic Kurds.

"While the revolution was still young, only eighteen months old, Saddam Hussein invaded Iran. Saddam was hoping to take advantage of the internal chaos created by the revolution. His invasion had the opposite effect. It brought the Iranian people together. It solidified Khomeini's leadership and unified the country in resistance.

"One day, Suleimani was sent to the front to supply water to the soldiers. It was a one-day mission, but once he got to the front lines, he refused to leave. Suleimani quickly earned a reputation for bravery and boldness. His specialty was reconnaissance missions behind Iraqi lines. He began to receive some acclaim after he returned from several missions bearing a goat, which his soldiers slaughtered and grilled. On Iraqi radio, Suleimani became known as 'the goat thief.' In recognition of his effectiveness, he was put in charge of a brigade from Kerman.

"The Iranian Army was badly overmatched by the Iraqi military. In desperation, its commanders resorted to crude and costly tactics. The Iranians relied on human wave assaults. They would send thousands of young men directly into the Iraqi lines, often to clear minefields under direct fire from Iraqi guns. The soldiers died at a horrendous rate. On at least one occasion, Suleimani himself was wounded. Still, he never lost enthusiasm for his work.

"In the 1980s, Reuel Marc Gerecht was a young CIA officer posted to Istanbul, Turkey. Gerecht's job was to recruit from the thousands of Iranian soldiers sent there to recuperate. Gerecht divided the veterans into two groups. The first group was the broken and the burned out, the hollow-eyed, the guys who had been destroyed. The second group was the bright-eyed guys who just couldn't wait to get back to the front. He put Suleimani in the second category—a true believer, a fanatic with a thirst for blood.

"In 1987, during a battle with the Iraqi Army, a division under Suleimani's command was attacked by artillery shells containing chemical weapons. More than a hundred of his men suffered the effects. Suleimani believes to this day it was the Americans who supplied those chemicals to the Iraqis. His hatred of America is genuine and intense."

"In 1998, Suleimani was promoted to lead the Quds Force. He has built the Quds Force into an organization with extraordinary reach, with branches focused on intelligence, finance, politics, sabotage, and Special Operations.

"The Quds headquarters is in the former US embassy compound in Tehran. The exact size of his force is unknown. Some estimates put it as high as twenty thousand members. His forces are divided between special operators who serve in combat units and intelligence agents who oversee foreign assets. Its members are selected for their skill and their allegiance to the doctrine of the Islamic Revolution as well as loyalty to the leadership.

"Fighters are recruited throughout the region, trained in Shiraz and Tehran, indoctrinated at the Jerusalem Operation College, in Qom, and then sent on months-long missions to Afghanistan and Iraq to gain experience in field operational work. They usually travel under the guise of Iranian construction workers.

"After taking command, Suleimani strengthened relationships in Lebanon, with Mughniyeh and with Hassan Nasrallah, Hezbollah's chief. By then, the Israeli military had occupied southern Lebanon for sixteen years, and Hezbollah was eager to take control of the country, so Suleimani sent in Quds Force operatives to help. In 2000, Israel withdrew, exhausted by relentless Hezbollah attacks. It was a major victory for the Shiites, and it served as a blueprint for the war against the Americans in Iraq.

"In 2004, the Quds Force began flooding Iraq with lethal roadside bombs that the Americans referred to as EFPs, for explosively formed projectiles. The EFPs fire a molten copper slug that's able to penetrate armor. EFPs began wreaking havoc on American troops, accounting for nearly twenty percent of all combat deaths in Iraq. EFPs can only be made by skilled technicians, and they were often triggered by sophisticated motion sensors. There was never any question where they were coming from.

"Suleimani's campaign against the United States crossed the Sunni-Shiite divide, which he has always been willing to set aside for the larger purpose of destroying Israel and the US. Iraqi and Western officials believe that, early in the US occupation of Iraq, Suleimani encouraged the head of intelligence for the Assad regime to facilitate the movement of Sunni extremists through Syria to fight the Americans. Quds have a history of cooperating with Al Qaeda.

"As it turned out, the Iranian strategy of enabling Sunni extremists backfired. The same extremists began attacking Shiite civilians and the Shiite-dominated Iraqi government. It was a prelude of the civil war to come and the ISIS caliphate. Suleimani wanted to bleed the Americans, so he invited in the jihadism, and things got out of control. In this way he can be called the father of ISIS.

"It was Suleimani who brokered the ceasefire in Iraq. He was able to convince Malaki to accept peace with the Shia militias in exchange for the withdrawal of all American Forces. This is why Malaki was always so insistent on the removal of US troops, a demand your president was only too happy to oblige in 2012.

"Despite all Suleimani's rough work, his image among Iran's faithful is that of an irreproachable war hero, a decorated veteran of the Iran-Iraq War, in which he became a division commander while still in his twenties. In public, he's almost theatrically modest. During a recent appearance, he described himself as the smallest soldier and, according to the Iranian press, rebuffed members of the audience who tried to kiss his hand. His power comes mostly from his close relationship with Khamenei, who provides the guiding vision for Iranian society. The supreme leader, who usually reserves his highest praise for fallen soldiers, has referred to Suleimani as a living martyr of the revolution.

"Suleimani lives in Tehran and appears to lead the home life of a bureaucrat in middle age. He gets up at four every morning and he's in bed by nine thirty every night. He has a loving wife, three sons and two daughters and is known to be a strict but loving father.

"Suleimani is a far more polished guy than most. He can move in political circles, but he's also got the substance to be intimidating. Although he's widely read, he has almost no formal education. He's very shrewd and a brilliant strategist. His tools include payoffs for politicians across the Middle East, intimidation when it's needed, and murder as a last resort. Over the years, the Quds Force has built an international network of assets, some of them drawn from the Iranian migrants, who can be called on to support missions.

"Suleimani has orchestrated attacks in places as far-flung as Thailand, New Delhi, Lagos, and Nairobi—at least thirty attempts in the past two years alone. The most notorious was a scheme in 2011 to hire a Mexican drug cartel to blow up the Saudi ambassador to the United States as he sat down to eat at a restaurant a few miles from the White House."

"Why hasn't Israel taken this guy out?" Pat asked.

"Why haven't the Americans?" Pini responded.

"I don't know the answer to either question," Pat replied.

"We've tried in the past. We have not succeeded. Now that he remains in Iran, it is nearly impossible. You sound like you're going to make another run at it."

"My focus at the moment is limited to the Hezbollah drug, guns and money-laundering business here in UAE. I'm told Suleimani has his hand in that as well."

"Anything Hezbollah is also Quds, and anything Quds is Suleimani."

"Can you point me to anyone to talk to who might have info on the Hezbollah operations here in Dubai?" Pat said.

"I can't give you a name right now, I'll get back to you as soon as I can."

"Should I be optimistic?" Pat asked.

"You have a lot of cachet at the moment. That business in Oman and Yemen meant a lot to my people. You should be hopeful."

Chapter 20

The next morning, Pat untied the *Sam Houston* while McDonald got the systems started. It was seven in the morning, and the only other people in the marina area were dog walkers and joggers. Pat hopped onto the deck as McDonald glided the *Sam Houston* out of the slip and into the waterway. The route to the Arabian Gulf involved maneuvering through a mile of narrow man-made waterways and included passage under three bridges. It was slow going, which afforded Pat the time to take inventory of his floating home.

The military equipment and his arsenal had already been moved to storage inside the Trident hangar at Al Dhafra Air Force Base. The empty cabinet space inside the bar next to the galley attested to how badly his liquor supply had been ravaged. The people at Gulf Craft were going to do a complete remodel, which meant they were going to gut the interior completely.

He emptied the safe inside his stateroom into a strongbox. The contents consisted of cash, stacks of euros and dollars, and credit cards. One of the five-gallon oil cans inside the engine room had a hidden cache containing passports and Canadian Gold Maple Leaf coins. He removed those items and placed them into the same strongbox and carried it up to the flybridge.

"What's that?" asked McDonald, pointing at the box.

"Some items I had stashed for emergencies," Pat replied.

"I thought we found all the weapons. It's a good thing our vehicles never get inspected when we go onto the Air Force base. You could start a war with what you carry around in this thing."

"It gives me a sense of security."

"What about that stuff?" McDonald said, referring to the box.

"It's another third of the trinity."

"The trinity?"

"Yeah, the three elements needed to survive in our business: guns, money and intel. Inside this box is the money. You already removed the guns, and as for intel, that always seems to be in short supply."

"Speaking of survival, I thought you were going to bring up the damage to your liquor cabinet."

"I can just imagine Migos's playmates mixing Coke with one of my thirty-year-old single malts while captivated by stories of his heroic adventures at sea."

"You're not wrong. Taking this boat away from him might be the worst thing ever to happen to his love life."

"I don't think love is the right word for it. Remind me to tell the folks at the boatyard to burn the sheets."

"What's the plan from here on? Going up against the commander of the Quds might be punching a little above our weight."

"It would be punching way above our weight. Our current assignment is much more limited. We're going to start taking pieces of the Hezbollah organized crime network off the table. I haven't figured out exactly how to start yet. I'm counting on Pini to point us in the right direction."

"Why the focus on Suleimani, then?"

"He's the guy at the top. Eventually, if we do our job well, he's going to counter. Stupid not to know more about him. Plus, if I ever get the chance to take him out, I will."

"How do the people back at Langley feel about that?"

"All the planets and moons would have to line up perfectly to create an opportunity good enough for the big bosses to approve."

"You're seriously considering it, then?"

"I'm hopeful. Until then, I'm going to stick to the mission we've been assigned. The guy lives and works in the old US embassy compound in Tehran. I'm not delusional enough to think going after him is even remotely within our capabilities."

"I'm glad to hear that."

"Relax. The operations for the next few months are going to be mostly local, more intel collection than direct action. Having you guys play high rollers in Dubai over the past couple of weeks wasn't deliberate, but it's going to help with our cover. We're going to infiltrate the dark side of the Dubai finance business. Having Migos and his two running buddies traveling in the same circles as those shady ostentatious peacocks is exactly what was needed. The uniform for the next while is going to be Brioni suits and Bentleys instead of multicam and body armor."

"I'm sure that's going to kill Migos, Jankowski and Burnia."

"If nothing else, it'll be amusing."

The team gathered in Pat's suite at the Address later that afternoon. The living room was barely large enough to accommodate all five men. The men sat in a circle around the coffee table. A large floor-to-ceiling window offered a view of the marina and the towering sixty-floor skyscrapers of the Jumeirah Beach Residence beyond. Pat straddled a wooden chair he'd taken from behind the desk and sat on it backwards with his arms on the top of the back rest.

"The people at Langley are very satisfied with the Yemen operation. The battle damage assessment confirmed all three missile systems were destroyed. You didn't have an easy task. Limited visibility, with only a sketch map and general coordinates to the launchers. Finding the right hill to blow up at such a distance took brains and judgment, so congratulations on a job well done," Pat said.

"Boss I have to admit, that was one of the toughest things I've ever had to do. You were danger close, well inside the blast zone. The whole time that bomb was in the air and I had my laser on the target, all I could think about was…was damn, if this takes out Pat, am I going to get paid next month?" Jankowski said, to the laughter of the rest of the team.

"When Jankowski starts to loosen up enough to make jokes, you know it's time to get back to work. Which is good, because we've been given a new mission. This one is going to take a lot of intelligence collection and is going to require more subtlety and finesse than what we're usually known for."

Migos looked at Burnia and Jankowski, whom he sometimes referred to as the bam-bam brothers. "You should consider sending these two redneck knuckle draggers back to Abu Dhabi," Migos said.

"Let me finish the brief before any questions or comments. The US is trying to rein in Hezbollah, who've become super aggressive in the past few years. It's been in the papers that Hezbollah has become active in the drugs and gun-selling business, and the last US administration gave them a pass on it for political reasons.

"Many of the financing and business deals for that Hezbollah enterprise are conducted in Dubai. Our job is to unearth the players and take them off the board." Pat paused before continuing.

"Unearthing them is not going to be easy. We have intel support from Langley, we have some sources inside the city, and we have Dave Forrest working on it with Clearwater. I'm confident in a matter of days, we'll be able to begin to develop a target list." He looked over at Burnia and Jankowski, who were sitting on the couch wearing track suits. Both were impassive, taking everything in. The epitome of quiet professionals.

"Your job is to blend in with the beautiful people of Dubai, so that when the time comes, we'll be able to operate successfully in this environment without drawing unwanted attention. Hitting a Hezbollah money launderer in downtown Dubai isn't easy. Doing it without getting caught by law enforcement is harder still. They have CCTV cameras everywhere, and the local government isn't keen on foreign operators interfering with the business of Dubai, which is shady finance. This place is the money-laundering capital of the world because the Dubai government wants it that way. Whatever we do, we need to make sure that above all else, we leave no trace." Pat walked over to a side table, where he picked up and opened a thick manila envelope.

"You four are going to stay at the Armani downtown. I'm going to be at the Fairmont on Sheikh Zayed Road. No special cover or IDs are needed. We're all Trident, and we're already weapons dealers. Continue to hang out with the beautiful people. Try to connect with others in the trade. Act and dress the part of a high roller. Maintain access to a vehicle and make sure you always keep a suppressed handgun nearby, but don't carry unless it's absolutely necessary.

"Burnia, your first task is to put together a team surveillance package—comms, trackers, sensors, the works. At some point we'll have to switch into tracking mode. Jankowski, you put together an assault package. Jessica has already booked your rooms. I have your reservations in this envelope. Your UAE bank accounts have been augmented for expenses. Play the part, but don't go too crazy. Do you have any questions?"

"Define too crazy," Migos asked.

"Don't buy exotic African cats, furs or Bollywood starlets. Don't charge me for expensive jewelry. Feel free to rent the most exotic car you can find, just don't buy it. Stuff like that."

"I can live with that," Migos said.

"Ostentatious behavior and conspicuous consumption are needed to blend in, so don't act like you're still in the military. Just remember, I send these bills to Langley, and I'd appreciate it if you don't make the billing process too painful."

"I'm renting a McLaren, is that okay?" Burnia asked.

"Perfectly okay. You may want to upgrade your wardrobe while you're at it. Nothing against your go-to blue jeans and t-shirts, but Dubai is not Silicon Valley. Our target audience leans more towards sports jackets and suits."

Pat checked out of the Address and moved to the Fairmont on Sheikh Zayed. He went up to the twenty-eighth floor and checked in at the Gold Club. He had been a regular at the Fairmont for years, and although it wasn't the Armani, he preferred the familiarity. His room had a view of the one-hundred-and-sixty-three-story Burj Khalifa, the tallest building in the world. The Armani Hotel occupied ten of the lower floors in the Burj. The reservations Jessica made for the team would give them club access on the one hundred and twenty-first floor, below the At.Mosphere restaurant and bar.

He quickly changed and headed to the ninth-floor gym. Another thing he liked about the Fairmont was the gym. It had free weights and great views, and the attendants left you alone. He finished on the treadmill, which overlooked the sunset pool. It was late afternoon, and the pool area was full of sunbathers and early drinkers who liked to sit at the edge of the infinity pool that overlooked the city.

The Fairmont was a city hotel that held little appeal to families. Most of the people around the pool were businesspeople and their companions. The happy couples lounging around the pool reminded him of Susu, so he turned the treadmill speed up to fourteen and returned his thoughts to running.

Pat got out of the Uber and entered La Petite Maison restaurant at the Dubai Financial Center. He was early, so he took a seat at the bar to the right of the entranceway. The dining room was full, which was normal for the renowned chain that specialized in French Niçoise cuisine. He ordered a glass of rosé and checked his phone for messages. Midway through his drink, Pini arrived. The two were escorted into the dining room by a blond Eastern European hostess who was almost as tall as him.

He ordered a bordeaux, a Château Figeac. The two men engaged in small talk until the appetizers arrived. On Pini's suggestion, Pat had the poulpe finement tranché, a very thinly sliced octopus cooked in lemon oil that was a house specialty.

"Any good news from your people?" Pat asked.

"You're to enjoy their full cooperation," Pini replied.

"Unlike you, I'm not a real intel guy. My methods are pretty basic. I usually just start with a string and then I pull it until I get to the end. What I don't have at the moment is that first string. I don't suppose you have anything to offer."

"I do. I have a very good starting point." Pini halted while the waiter stepped forward and refilled each of their wineglasses from the decanter.

"Mustafa Assad is a Lebanese national here on a UAE resident visa. He lives in Dubai. He's an arms broker, but he works the fringes. His biggest customers are in Libya, south Sudan and Lebanon."

"Who are his biggest suppliers?" Pat asked.

"Ukraine, Bulgaria, China and North Korea," Pini replied.

"I've never heard of him. Does he manage his own book or someone else's?" Pat asked.

"He has a patron, same person who sponsors his resident visa. Man's name is Mohammed Al Suedi. He owns several businesses in UAE."

"Him, I know. He owns an Abu Dhabi company, Emirates Defense Corporation. EDC has a very bad reputation."

"That's the one."

"They're blacklisted from doing business with the UAE armed forces. They have been for years, which probably explains why they've gone over to the dark side."

"Why were they blacklisted by the UAE GHQ?"

"The rumor is they sold a large order of ammunition they knew was bad. They did a factory acceptance test for a big order of RPGs in Czech and then, after the rounds were inspected and test-fired, they switched them out and shipped a load of Chinese RPGs that had a high misfire rate."

"Al Suedi is lucky he's not in jail."

"He has been, off and on, for a wide number of offenses. His dad is close with the top sheikhs—otherwise they would have thrown away the key."

"Have you met him?"

"Only once. He's a tall skinny kid with that vacuous drug addict look. He's a lightweight. Whatever Mustafa Assad is doing, I doubt Al Suedi is calling the shots."

The main course was a fourteen ounce rib eye steak that confirmed Pat's conviction that La Petite Maison had the best steak in Dubai.

"How do I find this Mustafa character?" Pat asked.

"He lives somewhere in the city. He's a partier. Most nights you'll find him either at Novikov or at Privé."

"What does he look like?"

"I'll send you a photo. He's overweight, dark curly hair, midforties, medium height. Very flashy—gold chains, the works. You'll have no trouble spotting him. He moves with an entourage."

The next night, Migos and Burnia went to Novikov and Jankowski and McDonald went to Privé. Neither team found him, so the next night they rotated locations. At half past ten in the evening, Pat received a text from Migos notifying him that the subject was at Novikov.

Pat took the elevator down to the lobby of the Fairmont, turned left and headed north along the sidewalk. The Sheraton was three buildings up from the Fairmont along the same city block. Novikov had an exterior door from within the hotel building. A huge Russian doorman blocked the entryway and ignored Pat as he stood behind the red velvet rope. Pat was wearing a black sports jacket, a gray button-down shirt and black trousers. He was sporting a gold Patek Philippe Grand Complications watch and thought he was dressed well enough to earn admission, but the doorman appeared unimpressed. After a fifteen-minute waiting period during which two other groups were ushered into the restaurant without delay, the doorman finally deigned to part the velvet rope and usher him into the rarified halls of Novikov.

The lounge was packed, and the cigarette smoke so dense it stung his eyes. A hostess dressed in black greeted him as he stepped inside, and his eyes began to adjust to the darkness. He gave the girl a pair of hundred-dirham notes and told her he was looking for his friends. Two Amerikis with huge biceps, he pantomimed. She smiled and led him across the lounge by the arm like a blind man to find Migos and Burnia.

There was a DJ playing loud electronic dance music somewhere in a corner. The hostess deposited Pat in a soft, deep chair next to a small round table with Migos and Burnia seated around it. A waitress came forward and mixed a gin and tonic from the bottle of Tanqueray already on the table.

"Where's our guy?" Pat asked.

"He's in the second-to-last booth against the wall at your three o'clock," Migos said.

Through the dim light, Pat was only able to see a group of six to eight men and women crowded inside a booth.

"How did you spot him? I could use a set of night vision goggles," Pat said.

"To get to the men's room, you have to walk right past that line of booths," Burnia said.

"What's the plan, boss?" Migos asked.

"Surveillance only. Let's see what kind of condition he's in when he leaves this place, and if he goes home alone or takes a companion. We need to know if he drives, takes a taxi or uses a service. It might take a few more nights before we get a feel for his routine, but once we do, we're going to grab him. Did you already text McDonald and tell him he could call it a night?"

"Yeah, we did."

Over the next two nights, they repeated the routine.

Mustafa Assad staggered out of Novikov at 2 a.m. His girl for the evening was talking to Migos, and Pat could see the anger on Mustafa's face through the rear seat window. Pat's black Mercedes 550 pulled up to the curb, and because he was distracted, Mustafa stepped forward, thinking it was his. When he noticed the car belonged to someone else, he turned to get back on the curb. The door to the backseat opened and before Mustafa could make it back onto the curb, Burnia and Jankowski closed on him from behind and pushed him into the backseat of the car. Jankowski jumped into the backseat and Burnia the front, and the car sped away. Mustafa's paramour missed the abduction, her view blocked by the annoying American with huge shoulders who refused to take no for an answer.

Pat and Jankowski flex-cuffed Mustafa's hands and feet and covered his mouth with a piece of duct tape. The heavy man was intoxicated and not a good physical specimen to begin with. In a full panic, he resisted as best he could, trying to throw elbows and head-butts, but he was no match for Jankowski and Pat, who easily restrained him.

They drove north, past the Dubai border and into the Northern Emirate of Sharjah. Pat had a rental workshop in the industrial section. It was nothing more than an open warehouse with dim lighting.

The next morning, Pat was alone with Mustafa. The heavy man was tied down to a heavy wooden door balanced on two milk crates that served as a fulcrum, allowing the door to seesaw. Pat removed the duct tape from the man's mouth and then tilted the door downward, dropping Mustafa's head to a position a foot lower than his feet.

Mustafa began to scream. Pat sat back and observed until the man tired and stopped yelling.

"You know what's coming—is that why all the yelling?" Pat asked.

"Who are you? Why are you doing this?"

"I need some information. I brought you here to get answers."

"You don't need to do this. I'll talk to you. What do you want to know?"

Pat moved the man to a chair and gave him some water. He turned on the digital recorder and took a seat on the stool across from Mustafa.

"How long have you been working in Dubai?"

"Seven years."

"What kind of work do you do?"

"I'm a trader, I buy and sell weapons."

"Who are your customers?"

"Governments. I sell to Africa and the Middle East."

"Do you sell to Lebanon?"

"Yes, I sell to the government of Lebanon."

"How do you get paid when you sell to Lebanon?"

"Wire transfer."

"Wire transfer from who?"

"From the Lebanese government."

"Where do you get your supplies? Who do you buy from?"

"Different countries."

"Government-owned companies or private?"

"Private."

"How do you pay for the weapons you buy?"

"Wire transfers."

"The same account as the one the buyers pay you with?"

"Yes."

"When you make these transactions, these wire transfers from buyers and wire transfers to sellers, what's the name of the company that owns the account?"

"The name of the company?"

"Yeah."

"It's a personal account. It's in my name."

"Why isn't it EDC?"

"It's just the arrangement we have."

"How does EDC get paid?"

"I make an annual payment to EDC for sponsoring me."

"What's the name of your bank?"

"Dubai Islamic Bank."

"I'm going to need your bank login information."

"I don't have it memorized. I can't give that to you."

Pat stood up, grabbed Mustafa by the throat and threw him back on the door. As he tied him down, Mustafa started screaming again. When Pat finished, he brought over a five-gallon pail of water and a towel.

Minutes later, Pat had the banking information and the passwords he needed. He started up his computer and logged in to Mustafa's bank account. It took him only a few minutes to find what he was looking for, but he went through the transaction records for more than six hours before returning Mustafa to the chair for a second round of questioning.

"For every buy transaction, there's a sell transaction. The difference in values is enormous. If this was a real business, your margins would be two to three thousand percent. You're just moving money though franchise operations in Europe and Africa to make it look legitimate and then routing the money back into Lebanon. That's not very imaginative. You must have very little respect for the authorities. Who came up with this idea, anyway?"

"It was mine."

"No, I don't think it was. I just transferred the balance of your account to a bank in the Caymans. Two hundred and forty-seven million dirhams. What happens next is up to you. I can release you, or I can turn you over to the custody of the US government. I'm pretty sure if I release you, nobody you work for is going to believe you didn't steal that money. You don't have a scratch on you. I don't think anybody will buy that you didn't give the money up willingly."

"I want US protection."

"I don't blame you. It's the only smart call."

"In exchange, I want the contact information of every person in your network."

***

After getting some rest, Pat met the team at Cin Cin bar on the mezzanine level of the Fairmont. The team was in good spirits.

"How's Mustafa doing?" asked McDonald.

"He's on an Emirates flight to Dulles as we speak," Pat replied.

"Seriously?" McDonald said in disbelief.

"Yeah, the USA gave him a better offer than any he was going to get from his previous employer, so he jumped ship."

"What's next?"

"We finally have some targets. Once the Clearwater guys do their thing and pinpoint the HVTs, we should be getting the green light from Langley to go into assault mode."

"Why do we need approvals?" McDonald asked.

"This project is being worked on from two angles. There's a law enforcement effort, and there's a counterterrorism effort, which we're working. Mike has to do some information sharing to make sure what we're doing isn't screwing up what the DEA and other agencies are doing and vice versa."

"How's it all going to work?" McDonald asked.

"We grabbed Mustafa, who's being cooperative. He's probably one of ten or twenty, possibly even thirty Hezbollah bankers in Dubai. When we grabbed him, he fingered a couple of wholesalers in Africa and Europe. We'll grab the distributors and hang them upside down, and hopefully they'll identify more of the bankers. We'll then go back to the bankers until they give up more of the distributors. We'll keep doing that, going back and forth between the bankers and the distributors, until we run out of bad guys. Wash, rinse and repeat. It's a pretty simple but time-consuming play. It's going to take a lot time to work through this."

"Do you think we can roll up the entire operation that way?" McDonald asked.

"We'll hopefully get a big chunk of it. Eventually, they'll figure out what we're doing and adapt."

The team sat in the cigar bar area in the back of the establishment. They were seated around a big black glass coffee table on thick couches and heavy leather chairs. It was early, and the bar was only half-filled. Piano music played in the background. Pat ordered a second bottle of wine and left for the men's room. When he returned, he found several attractive young ladies had joined the table.

"This was a business meeting," Pat said to Migos, who was seated next to him.

"Sorry, I thought we were done," Migos said.

"Well, we pretty much were."

"Now, I know why you chose the Fairmont," Migos said.

"I like the Fairmont because of the gym and the location. The five-star hooker experience was never a consideration," Pat said.

"These are working girls?" Migos said.

"Some people call this place Sin Sin instead of Cin Cin. Yeah, these girls only want you for your money. Which doesn't make them much different from the girls that you had on my yacht. These girls are just a little more transactional about it," Pat said.

Migos rudely shooed the girls away. He seemed offended his animal magnetism and charm weren't the reason for the girls' attraction. The other guys at the table laughed.

"Muy Muy Migos doesn't need to pay," he proclaimed for all to hear.

Chapter 21

Budapest, Hungary

Pat entered the Good Spirit Bar and was greeted by a slim dark-haired Hungarian waitress with a nose ring. She was dressed in jeans and a sleeveless black t-shirt that gave her elaborate arm tattoos maximum exposure. He asked for a table for two and was seated in the main dining room at a small two-person table against a wall across from the bar. It was late in the afternoon, and only a few of the barstools were occupied.

The room was dark, with a full-length bar that had an impressive display of spirits stocked behind it on small black-framed shelves. From his vantage point, he could see at the end of the bar a glassed-in room with a single table and surrounding shelves containing various whiskey bottles. He ordered a Flying Rabbit India pale ale and a deer ham plate and waited.

Pat kept an eye on the front doorway, the back half of the dining room behind him. He turned his seat towards the bar so he could observe the entire room. A waitress with large tortoise-shell glasses delivered his IPA in a bottle with a frosted glass on the side. The pleasant young lady, who appeared more wholesome than her counterpart, poured his beer and smiled. Pat attempted to smile back, but a stab of pain from his split lip ended the effort. He held the cold mug against his swollen mouth for a short while before taking his first big gulp.

Mike entered the restaurant and spotted Pat before he could be intercepted by the girl with the tats. He walked over and took the seat across from Pat, signaling to the waitress that he would have the same drink.

"Are you okay?" Mike asked.

"Yeah, I'm fine. It was a close call, but all is good," Pat replied.

A plate of cold meat and cheese was brought to the table and placed between the two men. Pat finished his beer and requested another.

"Where do you want me to start?" Pat asked.

"Start from when you arrived in Budapest," Mike replied.

"Walid Abboud gave up Laszio Endre. Clearwater found Laszio in Budapest and tied him to a shipping company that operates on the Danube. It's a Ukrainian company named JSC, with a warehouse and loading and unloading operations in the Port of Budapest.

"I went in as advance party to conduct the reconnaissance. I got here two week ago. The warehouse was where David Forrest said it would be. The profile was exactly the same as the last six distribution centers we've hit. I was able to trace Laszio from his home to the warehouse and all around town without too much difficulty. I gave the go order for the team to deploy, with the idea that we would snatch Laszio the next day and then hit the warehouse."

"So far so good," Mike said.

"Everything was on plan. Clearwater was doing most of the surveillance electronically. We had Laszio's communications and were tracking him from above. The team was on a private jet, fully loaded in tactical mode. I had the ground transportation we needed. The plan was to take him by surprise from his home.

"I went to lay eyes on him one last time. I can't explain it, except to say that his body language had changed. He was tense, looking over his shoulder. He behaved as if he was expecting something to happen at any moment. That something had to have been us. I made the abort call and turned the team around in midair."

"I had a flight out the next day. I was watching Laszio's apartment on a remote camera system from inside my hotel room when the door was busted open. The assaulters weren't Hungarian. I'm almost positive they were Iranians. They were fully geared up—MP-5s, ballistic protection, high-end stuff."

"Where are they now?" Mike asked.

"Dead. There were four of them. I left them in the hotel room," Pat said.

"What happened next?"

"I went after Laszio. By the time I got out of the hotel, he was being escorted out of the building by a personal security detachment. We had a bit of car chase. My rental Mercedes SUV and his BMW sedan had a pretty major collision. I T-boned his car and sent it into the river. Which is why my face looks like this. Laszio and his two Hungarian bodyguards are dead. I went back to his apartment and grabbed his laptop. David Forrest downloaded it remotely. Hopefully we'll get something we can work with from it."

"You were stalking Laszio, but Quds was stalking you?"

"Exactly, they were using him as bait."

"Do you think the last banker you grabbed in Dubai was a plant?"

"Maybe. It's just as likely they knew what it meant once he went missing. They may have laid a trap around every one of the distributors that banker was working with."

"What are you going to do now?" Mike said.

"We need to rethink our approach. We always knew they would catch on eventually. We have over a billion of Hezbollah cash in that Caymans account. We've definitely made a dent in their operation. I'm a little surprised it took them this long to figure out what was happening. That's half a year's receipts if they're making two billion per year as you say."

"Next time you figure out an operation is burned, you need to move yourself. You shouldn't have stayed in the same hotel. You're lucky you weren't killed."

"Yeah, I don't know what I was thinking."

"You and your guys have done good work. We've definitely reduced the flow of funds going to Hezbollah, but we need to find another way to maintain the pressure," Mike said.

"I don't have any good ideas at the moment. By now, I'm sure they've changed how they're moving the money. I doubt any of the bankers you have in custody will be of any value in the future."

"They'll definitely change their financial hub. Probably switch up everything," Mike said.

"That might be an opportunity, because that'll require hands on by the top guys instead of the cutouts we've been dealing with."

"They can change how they bank and who runs the distribution nodes, but they can't change the fundamentals of the heroin industry. It's always going to be easier to change the banks than it'll be to change the distro network."

"What do you mean?"

"Ninety-five percent of the world's heroin comes from poppies grown in Afghanistan. The product flows from Afghanistan to Pakistan, India, China, Russia, Ethiopia, Somalia, Turkey, Nigeria, West Africa and the Balkans. Hezbollah is a tiny fraction of the total trafficking network. They dominate the Iran, Turkey to Balkans route. I don't think it's possible for them to encroach on other people's territories. I think if we maintain the pressure in Turkey and in the Balkans, we can eventually shut them down. Iran is off-limits."

"Where does the stuff go after the Balkans?" Pat asked.

"Mexico, mostly. Hezbollah sells to the Mexican gangs, who then bring it into the US for retail."

"If it's all right with you, I'm going to give my guys some time off. I'm going to the Bahamas for some R&R," Pat said.

"How's your boat coming along?"

"Almost done. We need your analysts and Clearwater to come up with another thread to pull on. It's a shame, but this last one has run its course."

"That's okay, it's part of the business."

Chapter 22

Tehran, Iran

Major General Suleimani sat on the floor of his living room as his wife placed platters of vegetables, fish, rice, chicken and bread on a thick clear plastic covering that was spread over the rug. He lived in a modest house without any servants. Wearing loose-fitting black cotton pants and a matching long-sleeved shirt, the general could have easily passed as a shopkeeper or an office clerk. His three adult sons and his son-in-law chatted among themselves as they shared the meal with him. His married daughter, three daughters-in-law and seven grandchildren were all dining in an adjacent room. The only family member missing from the weekly holy day meal was his youngest daughter.

General Suleimani was in an angry mood. He was careful to mask his temper, since he took great pride in never displaying emotion. The latest news had been distressing. His daughter, who attended university in Malaysia, had been misbehaving again. The reports from his network of people who spied on her daily were worrisome. Her fondness for Western music and her willingness to socialize with men were becoming a source of great pain to him. He was sorely tempted to return her to Tehran but was worried about the long-term damage it would do to their relationship. She was his youngest, and perhaps he had doted on her too much.

News from Hezbollah was equally disappointing. The demands for money from Lebanon were unceasing. The government in Beirut was corrupt and had an insatiable appetite for funds. After launching the opening salvos of rockets at Tel Aviv, they had folded after the first counterstrike from the Israelis, and now they were begging for money to rebuild. It was only a matter of time before the Americans would reimpose economic sanctions on Iran. Funds were tight and getting tighter. Money from the only reliable Hezbollah revenue stream was drying up as the Americans continued to interfere with the drug business.

Because of operations in Yemen, Syria and Iraq, General Suleimani had precious little time to devote to the Hezbollah drug operation and was annoyed by the prospect of having to make time. The most recent loss of Quds Force members in Budapest had caused him to rethink his priorities.

His confidence that he would outwit the Americans had not been born of arrogance. His track record in Lebanon, Iraq and Syria over the past twenty-five years spoke for itself. His ability to defeat the Americans was never in doubt. The situation had become serious enough that he felt it now warranted his attention. He couldn't afford to make up the lost Hezbollah revenue from his budget.

Later, he would meet with his most trusted advisors. They would handpick teams to send to Dubai, Beirut, Hungary, Istanbul and Belgrade to evaluate the problem with the Hezbollah supply chain. They would identify the source of the CIA interference, and they would return to Tehran to develop a plan for his consideration on how to eliminate the problem.

Chapter 23

Eleuthera, Bahamas

The drive from the beach house to the Trident office in Governor's Harbour took only fifteen minutes. His office manager, Jessica, was standing by in the hallway of the converted house when he arrived. Jessica and two local Bahamian women managed the financial and administrative operations of Trident from the office on Queen Street. The office building was originally a two-story residence, a grand home built by a wealthy trader in the late nineteenth century. It was constructed in the style of the West Indies, with exterior stone walls covered with conch-pink stucco. White wooden storm shutters surrounded the windows, and four white pillars stretched from the ground to the roof in the front. Pat had completely renovated and modernized the house when he'd purchased it.

Governor's Harbour is a small town with a year-round population of barely over seven hundred. It has a ferry to Nassau and a small airport that makes travel to the mainland convenient. Fort Lauderdale is only two hundred and fifty miles by air. Another benefit of the office's location was that it was only a two-minute walk to the First Caribbean Bank.

Jessica greeted Pat with a hug as he entered the foyer. The tiny Korean American took Pat by the arm and led him up the stairs to her office, which was decorated in the colonial style, with dark hardwood paneling and furniture and a deep red carpet. The art consisted of period oil paintings of the island from the age of the tall ships. Pat always felt the office invoked a Pirates of the Caribbean theme.

The two sat and discussed the business and finances for several hours. Jessica was a high-strung woman who had command of every detail of the business. Pat had always found the nuts and bolts of the gun trade to be immensely boring. He found subjects like irrevocable letters of credit, performance bonds, export licenses and customs clearance procedures to be sleep-inducing. He always feigned interest in these periodic updates, though, because he recognized the benefit of allowing Jessica to show off her command of the company's operations and finances every once in a while.

Eventually the conversation shifted to Jessica's personal life. She was a young mother of two, a true tiger mom who brought the same level of intensity to parenting as she did to the business. Grooming toddlers for the Ivy League from the sleepy village of Governor's Harbour was no easy task, but Jessica was taking it on headfirst. Jessica had an education and development plan for her kids that made Operation Overlord look simple by comparison. Pat avoided discussion about Jessica's husband. He was a ne'er-do-well, with a reverse Midas touch for any business he came in contact with. Jessica and Pat both agreed that Jonathan would never have a role in Trident, despite his regular requests to become involved.

It was almost three in the afternoon when Pat returned to the beach house. When he entered the home, he was greeted by Maria at the entryway. She was dressed in a green muumuu with a band around her hair and a vacuum cleaner attachment in her hand.

"You have a guest in the living room. I informed her that you were not at home, but she insisted on waiting," Maria said.

"Who is she?" Pat asked.

"She didn't give me her name. She was certain you would want to meet her. That is what she said," Maria replied.

Pat was puzzled and a little curious. The living room was the least-used room of the house. It was at the end of a hallway on the first floor. The room was a formerly decorated parlor that had very little utility in a beach house. As he turned the corner to enter the room, he saw her and stopped dead in his tracks.

Susu stood and walked up to the speechless Pat and put her arms around him. Pat could feel her trembling as her tears soaked into the chest of his cotton polo shirt. Behind him, he heard Maria enter the room and quickly withdraw. Pat held Susu for as long as it took him to regain his composure, which felt like an eternity. When the frog finally disappeared from his throat and he felt he could speak, he led Susu to the couch and the two sat down.

Maria timidly poked her head into the room and then came forward, placing a tea service on the coffee table in front of the couch. Pat gripped Susu's hand tight, thinking it might be a good idea never to let go. After a long silence, Susu spoke.

"I'm sorry, it must have hurt you believing I was in the Chedi that night."

"Why didn't you send me a message?" Pat asked.

"I was on my way back to the Chedi when it was attacked. I must have arrived only moments later. Nobody knew where I was. My mission in Oman was finished. My career was finished. I was months from retiring. The fire was as an opportunity to get away from the Chinese government and be with you, so I took it."

"You left me to be with me?" Pat said.

"There was never any guarantee the Chinese government would let us be together. Once I retired, my passport would have been immediately confiscated and never replaced. I would never have been allowed to leave China again. Those are the rules for intelligence and military officers."

"We've discussed this many times," Pat said.

"I don't want to live in China, and I don't want the Chinese government to decide whether or not I can be with you. It was better that I died that night in the Chedi. Now, I can be with you, with no restrictions or conditions, forever," she said.

"Why did you wait so long? It's been months," Pat said.

"I had to create a new identity. I couldn't use anything or anyone I worked with in the past. Everyone I know would have been spied on by Chinese intelligence. I had to assure the Chinese government that I am no longer among the living."

"What now?" Pat said.

"Now my name is Cheryl Li. I'm from London, and I live with my boyfriend in the Bahamas."

"This is unbelievable," Pat said.

"Yes, it is," Susu/Cheryl said.

"Who can I tell?" Pat said.

"Nobody. I've never met Mike or any of your friends and workmates. Introduce me as Cheryl and leave it at that."

"Mike will figure it out," Pat said.

"Of course he will, but he will never reveal our secret. He's too loyal a friend."

"Do you have any baggage? You're staying here from now on, right?"

"Yes, of course. I don't have any baggage. I'm poor. I spent all my money on identifications and travel. You might need to take me shopping."

"Tomorrow, we'll go to Nassau and shop. Let me take you around and introduce you to the household. Are you hungry?"

The late winter weather was in the low eighties and sunny. Pat had considered the ferry but rethought the idea when he realized it was a five-hour trip. The twin-engine Cessna charter from Governor's Harbour Airport was far more convenient.

It was a picturesque trip. A car was waiting for them when they landed. On the way back, the packages barely fit inside the airplane. The trip to Crystal Court inside the Atlantis Hotel was a new experience for Pat. After thirty minutes of power shopping, he retreated to a coffee shop and returned to Cheryl only when she texted him that his debit card was needed.

Cheryl was extraordinarily pleased with her clothing, shoes, bags, hats and jewelry choices. The idea amused Pat, who had thought such things were beneath the former Mata Hari. When they returned, she raced to the bedroom and tried all her clothes on all over again and then gave Pat a mini fashion show.

"That was so much fun, thank you," Cheryl said.

"That's a side of you I've never seen before, the happy shopper."

"That's a side I expected of you. I'll bet that's the most time you've spent in a mall in years."

"It is, and in the future, you can do your own shopping. Tomorrow we'll go to the bank and get you set up with some spending power," Pat said.

"The Chinese government is very stingy with funds. The salaries are modest. Most people who work for the government make their money through corruption. High-ranking intelligence officers are rarely corrupt. If we build savings, the government thinks we're being paid by our enemies for information. It's a good way to wind up in prison. We're the only poor people in government," Cheryl said.

"You're not poor anymore," Pat said.

"If you give me money, I want to earn it," Cheryl said.

"That's why I kept telling you to go into the Victoria's Secret," Pat said.

"That's not funny. I don't want to be your kept woman," Cheryl said.

"You're my partner. I'll take good care of you," Pat said.

"I want to work. I can help with Trident."

"The CEO job is filled and so is the office manager position. What do you have in mind?"

"Strategy, planning, intelligence collection and analysis. Those are my strengths. I know you have David Forrest, but the work he does is technical, not refined analysis. You need someone on your team with my skills."

"You're not going out into the field ever again. You can live comfortably here for the rest of your life. Don't worry about money. I have a lot, and this time tomorrow, it won't be a problem for you anymore either."

"I don't intend to go back out into the field. What I'm talking about is helping you from the back office."

"I don't need any help."

"I saw those scars on your back when you got out of bed this morning, Pat. You need my help."

"You think you would have prevented them?" Pat said.

"I don't know how you got them but, yes, I probably could have. I want to protect you the same way you want to protect me. Let me do what I've been trained to do."

"You are pretty good at your job, even if Oman was a disaster."

"Is the sultan still named Asaad?"

"Yes."

"Then Oman wasn't a disaster. Mission accomplished. Not my fault the US can't control the ayatollahs. My job was to elect Asaad and to protect Chinese investments," Cheryl said with a pout.

"I need permission from Mike to read you in on current operations. He'll approve, but I'll need to talk to him about this in person."

"That's fine. I've already made an appointment for you to see a doctor in Miami. Afterward you can go to Virginia and meet Mike."

"Who's the appointment with?"

"A top plastic surgeon in Miami. He's going to make those scars on your back disappear. I don't like them," Cheryl said.

"I'm not a fan either."

"I can tell. We'll make you pretty again very soon."

"Pretty?"

Pat flew private from Miami to Dulles and took a room in Tysons Corner. The limo dropped him in downtown Culpepper at an old two-story brick building with a Piedmont Steakhouse sign on the front. Culpepper was off the beaten path for the Langley crowd, which was always a requirement for a meeting with Mike.

Pat found Mike upstairs seated next to the window. He had already ordered a bottle of red wine, and his glass was half-empty. Pat slid into the seat, and the waitress immediately swooped in with a menu. Not in the mood for wine, Pat ordered the James Bond 007 Martini and the fried dill pickles.

"007 Martini, seriously?" Mike asked.

"Just trying to live up to the hype." The two chuckled.

When his martini was delivered, he took a sip and then requested a wineglass.

"What's wrong?"

"I Just remembered why I don't drink martinis. They taste like gasoline."

"Any new developments on the counterdrug operation?" Mike asked.

"No, we're out of leads. I was hoping you had something."

"Not yet. We're continuing to squeeze the prisoners, and we have people in the field collecting, but we don't have anything actionable yet."

"I want to augment my team with someone who I think could help."

Mike's attention intensified, reminding Pat once again that he had the worst poker face in the world.

"Who?"

"Susu."

"She's alive?"

"She was on her way back to the Chedi when she saw it inferno, and she took advantage of the opportunity to shake her employer," Pat said.

"Now she wants to work for us?"

"She wants to work with David Forrest and add another dimension to the analysis and planning part of our business."

"She could definitely provide something you lack. No offense. The question is, can we trust her?" Mike said.

"I'd bet my life on it," Pat said.

"That's the point, you will be. And if it was just your neck on the line, this would and should be solely your call. Trouble is, the linkage with the Agency creates some exposure."

"I know. That's why I'm here asking for permission."

"Can I talk with her?"

"Yeah. I have a plane. Why don't we finish dinner and then fly back to Governor's Harbour so you can interrogate the love of my life?"

"You're flying out of Dulles, private?"

"Yes," Pat replied.

"Okay, we can swing by my place on the way and I'll pick up some things." The meals arrived, and the discussion shifted from business to family and the upcoming baseball season. They both had the bone-in rib eye, which was a carnivore's wet dream.

"Good choice on the wine, by the way. This Duckhorn cabernet is a perfect match," Pat said.

"When I dine with you, expense is never an issue. I like to splurge. Don't forget to pick up the check." The two laughed.

Chapter 24

Kermanshaw, Iran

General Suleimani walked up the steps of the Parsian Hotel in Kermanshaw. The hotel was familiar to him. He had stayed in the exact same hotel in 1981, the last time the ayatollahs had tasked him with suppressing a Kurdish uprising. The flight from Tehran to the farthest city west along the Iraqi border had taken only three hours, and Suleimani was anxious to get to work. The top two floors of the six-story hotel had been commandeered by the Quds Force.

He was escorted to the largest suite on the top floor. The officers assembled in a circle in the living area came to their feet at the arrival of the general, and with a gesture, he asked them to sit while he occupied a chair off to their side. Black tea was served. The general remained silent while the officers around him carried on with side conversations. General Suleimani sat quietly observing for many minutes while he finished his tea. With an almost imperceptible nod, he signaled his loyal deputy, Hossein Hamadani, to begin the meeting.

"Sir, we are graced by your presence. We praise Allah for your safe passage to Kermanshah, and we beg for your wisdom to guide us through these difficulties. We will begin with a saying of the Quran, and then Colonel Farhad will brief you on the intelligence situation."

A bearded imam replaced the deputy at the front of the room and began with the Isti'aathah, saying in Arabic, "I seek refuge in Allah from the Accursed Satan." The assembled officers held their hands folded in front of them in prayer and then dropped their heads and simulated washing their faces before the imam began to sing the Quranic verse. The imam finished after several minutes and returned to his seat, Colonel Farhad taking his place.

"Your excellency, Kermanshah is the ninth-largest city in Iran and it has a majority Kurdish population. The major industries are agriculture, textiles and manufacturing. The largest employer is the Kermanshah oil refinery. The people here are blessed with a strong economy and good sources for food and shelter.

"Despite the many blessings bestowed upon the people of Kermanshah, there has been a serious protest movement within the city for many years. The city has a population of nine hundred thousand, and during the Green Movement in 2009, more than one hundred and fifty thousand marched against the government. The police and military responded swiftly in 2009, arresting the rebel leaders and rooting out the traitors. The military response to the protest marches was swift and harsh, and for almost nine years we had few problems.

"December was the anniversary of the Green Movement protests, and in 2017, we began to see further examples of dissent. Once again, the police and military have been aggressive in detaining and interrogating the traitors, but no matter how much the pressure is increased, the protests continue to grow.

"Our suspicion is that there is a Zionist cell operating within the city. We believe the Zionists and the Americans are fueling this dissent. Despite all our efforts to uncover this cell, we have as of yet produced no results. We await your wisdom and guidance on how to proceed."

General Suleimani did not speak. He thought about the words of the colonel, which effectively said nothing constructive about the problem. The ayatollah had called him and asked him personally to address the situation of unrest in Kermanshah. If he had to, he would line up every man, woman and child in the city and execute them. But first he thought it prudent to talk with some of the prisoners and city leaders.

"Thank you for the excellent briefing. You are dismissed." General Suleimani then stood up and asked his deputy to assign him to a smaller, simpler hotel room.

Chapter 25

Paphos, Cyprus

The recently appointed chief intelligence officer at Clearwater called a team meeting at the company office in Paphos, Cyprus. Pat, McDonald, Migos, Burnia and Jankowski arrived on a company C-130. The Clearwater office was a walled-in section of the Trident hangar, which was located in the cargo section of the Paphos airport.

The Trident hangar was huge, capable of housing two C-130s. Half of it was used for storage. On one side was a sizeable inventory of tactical vehicles, equipment and gear. Inside one of the secured rooms was an extensive armory of weapons and munitions. Two adjacent offices had been assigned to Clearwater, the private intelligence firm led by David Forrest. Pat could see signs of recent renovations on the Clearwater side of the hangar, and he was interested in seeing what had been done.

Pat spotted the portly David Forrest at the entryway to the Clearwater offices. The hangar doors were open, and the warm salt air of Paphos flowed into the building along with the whine of the C-130's engines shutting down. Despite the heat, David Forrest wore a three-piece suit. He held an unlit pipe that rarely if ever left his possession. The normally unkempt professor had his white beard and mustache neatly trimmed and his tie straight. The professor greeted each of the team members and held the door open as he ushered them in.

The Clearwater office had changed dramatically since Pat's last visit. The space had transformed from a utilitarian space that had housed a Cray supercomputer, routers, advanced communications gear and workstations to a professional office that had the look and ambience of a high-end law office. The carpet was deep blue, the walls were white ash, the art was a series of Asian watercolor landscapes, and the lighting was subdued.

The group passed through an exterior sitting room and entered a corridor, where they found a conference room behind the only open door. The conference room was purely high-tech. Big-screen computer monitors completely covered three of the walls. Around the mahogany conference table were ten black leather seats.

The men all sat down, with Pat at the end of the table. Coffee and donuts were served. Cheryl entered the room behind Pat. He was eating a jelly donut and wasn't aware she had entered the room until he saw the head of every man in front of him turn. She walked to the end of the table and introduced herself.

"Good morning, gentlemen. My name is Cheryl Li. I'm the CIO at Clearwater, and I'll be giving you the intelligence update this morning." Cheryl smiled. She was wearing an off-white sleeveless silk shirt and matching skirt that highlighted her tiny waist, ample breasts and toned physique. She wore no jewelry and only light makeup. Her brunette hair was shoulder length and parted on the side, with a trace of curls. Her face was flawless and perfectly symmetrical, oval-shaped with high cheekbones, a delicate chin, large almond-shaped brown eyes, a smallish, perfectly straight nose and full lips. Pat was mesmerized. He had barely enough self-awareness to realize that concentration during briefings was going to be a problem as he sipped his coffee to compensate for the sudden dryness in his mouth.

Pat was hypnotized for the next sixty minutes while Cheryl presented a history of Kermanshah, Iran, Quds and Major General Suleimani. The final twenty minutes of the briefing dealt with translated communications intercepts and satellite and UAV video coverage of Major General Suleimani.

"Gentleman, we have a real-time confirmed fix on the Quds commander. He's located in Kermanshah, Iran. His current residence is the Parsian Hotel, and based on his current assignment, which is suppression of the local Kurdish protest movement, we anticipate he will remain in the area for another week. What are your questions?"

David Forrest was beaming. Migos, Burnia and Jankowski appeared stunned. Neither spoke or moved. McDonald looked perplexed, tapping his fingers against the table, looking up as if to summon a thought.

"What's the mission?" McDonald finally asked.

"We're going to kill the Quds commander," Pat said.

"If the Americans know where he is, they should just launch a Tomahawk missile and be done with it," McDonald said.

"They want deniability. Assassinating the Quds commander is an act of war," Pat said.

"More of this proxy shit. The Iranians use Houthis to launch a ballistic missile at the Saudi king, and the Americans use Trident to kill the Quds commander," McDonald said.

"Now you get it," Pat said.

"So, what's next?" McDonald asked.

"Dave, we need more information. Can you plot the air defenses around Kermanshah and then due west all the way to the Iraq border? We also need as much info as possible on that hotel and who else is in it. We need to know where the quick reaction forces are located that would respond to an attack on the hotel. We don't have the green light to take out Suleimani yet, but if we can present a viable plan, I'm pretty sure we'll get it. Dave give us what you have on the ADA and the hotel at six tonight. I have a concept that I'll brief afterward, and then you guys can poke holes in it and improve it until we have something operational that will work."

Pat stood up and left the room. He kept a small private office in the hangar that bore a much closer resemblance to what one would normally expect to see in a hangar, versus the modernized Clearwater side of the building. He called Mike.

"I know it's the middle of the night, but I wouldn't be calling at this hour if it wasn't important," Pat said.

"What do you need?"

"We have a location for Suleimani. He's at a hotel in Kermanshah, and he's expected to stay there for at least a week. It's right on the Iraqi border. I want permission to take him out."

"Do you have a plan?"

"I'm working on it. I also need some equipment rushed out to Paphos ASAP."

"What kind of equipment?"

"I need one AH/6S and one MH/6S. The MELB un-manned versions, complete with ground control station. Make sure the GCS has the sim package. My guys will need some practice."

"What for?"

"I need them for the Iranian leg of the journey."

"I can do that. I'll issue the ship instructions now. It's going to take at least a day to get a go or no-go decision."

"Understood. I'll operate as if the answer is yes, up until launch."

Chapter 26

Kermanshah, Iran

General Suleimani toured the detention facility with the local police commander. The interrogation rooms he inspected were blood-spattered dungeons that smelled of sweat and urine. The place he was currently inspecting was no different. A man so young he had only a wisp for a beard was strapped into mounts on the floor and ceiling in a standing spread eagle position. The man was naked, unconscious and caked in blood.

"What have you learned from this man?" Suleimani asked the police commander, who immediately referred him to the police captain who was running the interrogation.

"This man participated in the protest. He has given us the names of his associates who also marched," the captain said.

"What about the protest organizers? Did he know who they were?" Suleimani asked.

"No, he did not."

"Play me the recording of the interrogation. I want to hear how he responded to that question."

"I did not ask it, sir," the captain replied sheepishly after a long pause.

"Commander, all you are accomplishing here is punishing the protestors. Which is not a bad thing. But we need to focus on the organizers and the foreign influencers. Your people have shown that they are not up to that task. I am going to assign a team of Quds to advise your people. They will make you much more effective. Do you have any objections to that?"

"No, sir."

"The team will report directly to me, and you will report directly to them."

"Yes, sir."

"It's getting late. Tomorrow we'll continue with the police stations on the eastern side of the city."

Major General Suleimani had been working eighteen hour days for a week. He asked his driver to take him back to the hotel room. He had several reports to complete before retiring for the night, and he was anxious to get on with it. He was debating whether or not he should include the real reason the protests had grown to such a critical level. The problem in Kermanshah was the same problem Iran had with all of its security forces—a lack of talent and motivation. Officers were selected based on nepotism, patronage and revolutionary zeal without ample consideration given to brains and talent. The Quds Force was the lone exception.

***

The Hercules bounced through the rough air one hundred feet above the dark desert floor. The aircraft had been flying NAP of the earth for the past hour, ever since it had entered Kuwaiti and now Iraqi airspace. Pat, Migos, Burnia and Jankowski were all wearing static line parachute rigs. None of the team were wearing reserve parachutes. At three hundred feet, there wasn't going to be enough time to deploy one if the main failed.

The plane made a sudden climb to jump altitude, and the green light next to the cargo door turned on. Sachse signaled Pat to jump, and the four men handed their static line to Sachse as they filed off the cargo ramp into the night sky. It took only five seconds from when the parachute opened to when he hit the ground. He hit the ground first with his feet and finishing with his head slamming against a big rock. Thankfully, he hit the rock square with the latest in ballistic protection.

The weather was cool and dark, with little wind and a clear night sky. Pat marked one side of the road with IR ChemLite bundles while Migos marked the other side of the road. They were ten miles south of the Iraqi town of Mandali and less than ten miles from the Iranian border. Even though road traffic was deemed to be very unlikely, Burnia and Jankowski were on each end of the makeshift landing strip with an AT-4, an 84mm disposable antiarmor rocket. It was their job to stop any road traffic should it be needed.

The C-130J touched down, reversed thrust and braked to a fast stop. At the last runway marking, it did a pivot turn and dropped its ramp. Pat and Migos were the first up the ramp, followed by Burnia and Jankowski. Sachse already had the tie-downs released on the cargo. The men rolled the first little bird helicopter down the ramp and onto the road. Then they went back up and repeated the process with the second aircraft. The rotor blades were stowed on top of each other for shipping and had to spread out, positioned and locked down. The guns needed to be loaded and cycled and the aircraft powered up. Sachse supervised the building of the aircraft. Once the system check was complete and positive control was reported from the ground control station in Paphos, he retreated back inside the C130.

Pat sat forward on the MH-6's exterior seat above the right skid and secured himself with a retaining line he connected to the aircraft with a small carabiner. The tiny remotely piloted helicopter had four passengers, two on each exterior bench seat. He dropped his night vision goggles down in front of his eyes and waited for Migos to join him. Once Jankowski and Burnia reported set, Pat radioed McDonald to launch from the ground control station in Paphos.

The MH-6 looked like an insect with its big bubble windshield and protruding sensor array. It lifted into the air, and the AH-6 little bird gunship followed seconds later. The two aircraft headed due east to Kermanshah at an altitude of one hundred feet. At sixty knots, the wind in Pat's face was brisk. He pulled his neck gator up over his lower face. The hills west of Kermanshah peaked at five thousand feet; the hills east of Kermanshah were twice that elevation. The night air was cutting through Pat, who was in the forward seat, acting as a wind break for Migos, who huddled behind the bigger man to stay warm.

McDonald announced over the radio that the Hercules was airborne. It was heading south to safety, out of Iraqi airspace. Pat could picture McDonald and Cheryl sitting next to each other in the twenty-foot container that served as the GCS (ground control station) and control room inside the Paphos hangar. The display screen in front of them had the avionic and navigational information for their respective aircraft as well as a panoramic FLIR camera feed that allowed them to see where they were flying. McDonald's system also had sensor and optic feeds for the AH-6 weapons systems. On the big wall in front of them, they had a real-time satellite feed of the hotel and surrounding area.

The aircraft were being flown by the GCS computer. A detailed navigation route was plotted based on very accurate terrain data. Cheryl and McDonald were redundant, up until a change of the preprogrammed route was needed or, in the case of McDonald, whenever the GAU-19 50-caliber Gatling gun or the advanced precision kill weapon system (APKWS) rockets were needed for close air support.

The sixty-minute route into Kermanshah was an aerial roller-coaster ride as the aircraft hugged the uneven ground.

The computer controls were precise in maintaining an altitude of exactly one hundred feet over the terrain. The lights of the city were below them. Up ahead, Pat could see the river that marked the last reference point before the landing zone.

"Thirty seconds," McDonald's voice came over the radio.

Pat unhooked the retained line that connected him to the aircraft. He watched the AH-6 break formation as it moved into an orbit above the hotel in a low-level combat air patrol. The MH-6 flared as it descended onto the roof of the Parsian Hotel. All four men jumped off as soon as the aircraft got within a few feet of the building, and no sooner were they off than it leapt up and joined the AH-6 in a loitering pattern over the hotel.

As he approached the door to the roof, Pat readied his carbine. He was carrying a Daniel Defense Blackout 300 carbine with an integrated suppressor system and a 40mm M203 grenade launcher attached under the barrel. He heard the whoosh of the AH-6 unleashing an APKWS rocket. The missile struck an electrical transformer located five hundred meters from the hotel. After the boom of the rocket explosion, the city block went black. The APKWS was a precision laser-guided missile system that used the same cylindrical hydra rocket pods as the old unguided 2.75-inch rockets.

As soon as the neighborhood went dark, the roof door exploded from a breaching charge. The four men entered the stairwell from the roof, with Jankowski leading and Pat in the trail.

Even from inside the building, Pat could hear the GAU-19 dispatching the security forces positioned in vehicles outside the building. He was fourth in line running down the stairs when he heard the thud of the stairwell door being kicked open and then the mechanical sound of Jankowski's suppressed weapon discharging. The hotel had fifteen guest rooms on the sixth floor and eighteen on the fifth. Once Pat reached the stairwell exit, he followed Migos to the right. Burnia and Jankowski had already gone left. At the first door, Migos unslung his M3 Binelli shotgun and blasted the lock with a breaching round. Pat kicked in the door, tossed a flash bang, gave it three seconds to explode and followed it into the room as it was still going off in a series of blinding flashes and explosions. A disoriented Quds soldier was barely out of his bed when Pat shot him with his laser-aimed carbine.

Clearing the top floor was slow work. It took twenty minutes to reach the VIP suite where Pat expected the general to be staying. Migos blasted the door lock, and a fusillade of bullets came at them through the door from the inside. Pat kicked the door in and threw a flash bang. They found the combination living room and dining room area empty. Pat followed Migos down a corridor, and then the two split up, each taking a bedroom. Pat kicked in the thin wooden door and tossed in a grenade, only this time he threw in an M67 frag grenade. Migos did the same. The thick hotel plaster walls absorbed the shrapnel from the explosion. The two men then entered their respective rooms simultaneously. Pat found two men wounded and immobilized on the floor. Neither fit General Suleimani's description. He shot them both.

The plan had allowed a total of forty minutes to clear both floors. Pat checked his watch and noticed the top floor alone had taken thirty minutes. The two teams entered the stairwell in a stack formation and moved down to the fifth floor. With Burnia in the lead, the team reached the stairwell exit. Before exiting the stairwell, Burnia and Jankowski threw frag grenades into the hallway. Immediately after detonation, the two teams exited in opposite directions.

McDonald reported on the radio, "QRF destroyed. APKMS is Winchester, down to three hundred rounds on the fifty," which reminded Pat that they were behind schedule and needed to speed things up.

The two teams continued to clear the fifth floor. Unlike the sixth floor, the occupants of the fifth floor were alert and ready. The assaults became less precise and more firepower intensive. The M203 launcher under Pat's carbine became his go-to weapon as he began to clear rooms with flash bangs, then 40mm shotgun-like flechette blasts from his M203, followed by bullets from his carbine when necessary.

The air in the hallway was smoky and filled with dust. Pat's eyes stung, and his night vision was seriously degraded due to the smoke created by the fires from the munitions. Pat and Burnia had just cleared the last guest room on their side, and they still hadn't found any Iranian bearing even a slight resemblance to General Suleimani.

"No joy. Burnia, what about you?" Pat said over his radio.

"Negative," replied Burnia.

"No way he got past us and escaped. He's hiding somewhere. Burnia and Jankowski, you search the utility closets on the fifth. We'll take the sixth."

"Wilco."

Pat and Migos ran up the stairs to the sixth floor.

"You take left, I'll take right," Pat said as they entered the hallway.

With the smoke and dust, it was slow going finding any crawl spaces and closets Suleimani might have ducked into. After checking the entire hallway, he found only one closet, and the door was locked. Unlike the guest room doors, which opened in, the utility closet door opened out. Kicking it in was not a possibility. Pat removed the halogen tool he had attached to the back of his plate carrier. He slung his carbine over his shoulder and used the crowbar at one end of the tool to make a gap large enough to fit the right-angle wedge in. When the metal door was bent in enough, he inserted the right-angle wedge, and with his feet planted against the door, he pulled backward with both hands, forcing the metal door to open.

With all his weight and force pulling backwards, Pat suddenly found himself airborne, falling backwards, as the door opened. The general was standing in the closet doorway, silhouetted by the smoke and dust, with a pistol blasting away into the darkness around him in rapid fire. Still on his back, Pat threw the heavy steel halogen tool at Suleimani. The tool bounced off the general's chest. Pat was up and on Suleimani before he could recover and reaim the pistol.

When Pat's two hundred and fifteen pounds of lean muscle met the older and softer Suleimani's one hundred and forty pounds, it was no match. Pat wrestled the wiry little man onto his back and, sitting on his chest, leaned on his throat with his elbow and forearm until the smaller man stopped squirming. When he sat up and released the pressure on his throat, the general sprang up and flailed at him with his fists. Pat hit the general with a straight right, driving the flat of his hand into the tip of his nose. He heard a loud thud as the general's head slammed back against the tile floor. Pat sat up and looked down through his night vision at Suleimani's open-eyed dead man stare. The blow must have driven the other man's nose bone into his brain, killing him instantly.

Out of breath, Pat got on the radio. "Jackpot. Move to extraction point." Taking a device that looked like an iPhone out of his cargo pocket, he photographed Suleimani and captured his fingerprints.

The MH-6 was already on the rooftop when they arrived. The four men hopped into the same seats they'd used on the way in, and the little bird took off.

The two helicopters headed west, away from the city towards Iraq. Even though it was the same route at the same speed, the trip felt like it took twice as long. Pat spent the entire time waiting to be pounced on by the Iranian Air Force. He reminded himself that because of their small size and low altitude, it would have been very difficult to acquire the little birds on radar.

The C130 was already positioned to take off when they landed in Iraq. The four men quickly broke down the little birds and rolled them onto the aircraft. The tension didn't leave Pat's system until the pilots returned the Hercules to cruise altitude and announced they were out of Iraqi airspace.

The physical and emotional letdown from the mission was beginning to settle in. Pat and the other guys set up hammocks across the cargo compartment and went to sleep. The plane landed at Al Dhafra Air Force Base to refuel and went on to Paphos the next morning. A ground tug brought the C130 inside the hangar. Pat didn't want to offload the little birds without overhead cover to screen them from Russian satellites. He hoped the Iranians and Russians would trace the aircraft to the UAE and credit them with the hit as a reprisal for the cruise missile episode.

Chapter 27

Malta

The weather in Malta was unseasonably cool. Pat opened the salon door only partially to greet his guest.

"Come on in, Mike."

"Are you going to give me the tour? It looks like a brand-new boat."

"They did an amazing job. Sure, let me show you around."

When they got to the owner's stateroom, they caught Cheryl exiting the room. She was dressed in fashionable spring attire despite the weather.

"Where are you going, girl?" Pat asked.

"I have a hair appointment," she said.

"Will you be back for lunch?"

"No. I'm going to the spa, then shopping, I'll meet you two for dinner. I made reservations at seven at Chukkas. See you then."

"She seems happy."

"We both are."

"She's good at her job. She's the one who discovered General Suleimani, isn't she?"

"David and Cheryl work miracles together. Her insight into the human dimension and his science are a deadly combination."

"Her insight, as you call it, is a bit unnerving."

"She has something. Beyond her ridiculously amazing looks that seem to make anyone with XY chromosomes behave awkwardly, it feels like she's looking right through you."

"She's not a mind reader, is she?"

"You're not the only one who acts prepubescent around her. I think she's the sexiest woman alive."

"I'm glad you're happy. How has that testosterone-laden team of yours taken to her?"

"At first, Migos laid on the charm, to no effect. So, naturally, he's concluded she's gay. Burnia, Jankowski and McDonald love her. They came out of the Tier 1 environment where every plan and every potential contingency for every plan was studied and war-gamed to death. Trident's seat-of-your-pants style is a big adjustment for them. Having a first-rate intel officer on the team means a lot, brings Trident closer to their comfort zone," Pat said.

"Does anyone know where she came from?"

"She's very tight-lipped and secretive around the crew. They all think she's ex-CIA, and nobody is discouraging them from that conclusion."

"Do you think they'll ever figure it out?"

"She's a pro. She'll never slip. I'm the weak link, but I'm never going to say something that could endanger her. So, no, I don't think so."

"You're still working on the Hezbollah project, are you not?"

"Yes, we are. Although we're not making much in the way of progress, which is why I decided to go sailing to clear my mind."

"Where are you heading?"

"Canary Islands."

"Nice."

"How did the Iranian mission go over with the deep staters in swampland?"

"Very well. Lots of kudos. Suleimani bruised a lot of egos over the years. The way he was taken down has a lot of people scratching their heads. Folks didn't think such a thing was possible. You guys settled some scores and made it look easy."

"Easy is not how I would describe it. We have a solid team, lots of good ideas and a strong appreciation of what everyone adds to the group."

"The director wanted me talk to you about something else."

"What's that?"

"It's about that billion you took off Hezbollah."

"It's the Agency's billion. It's still in the same account in the Caymans."

"He wants you to hold on to it for a while longer. He's going to use it to fund projects he wants to keep off the books."

"I can arrange for someone else to have signature authority on the account. If the IRS finds out, I'm going to have a serious tax problem. I'd rather just turn it over to the government, to tell you the truth."

"Why don't you declare it as income and pay taxes on it?"

"I can do that, but it'll reduce the balance to about a billion dollars even, if that's okay with you."

"How is that possible?"

"How is what possible?"

"How can you pay taxes on a billion dollars and still have a billion left?"

"If I pay taxes on it, I'll be turning a billion euro into a billion USD."

"Wow, that's sweet."

"If you're feeling generous about your windfall, you can buy me those two unmanned little birds. Those are very useful systems."

"Wouldn't you prefer pilots?"

"In some situations, pilots are better. The cool part about those aircraft is you can use them both ways, with and without pilots."

"Are you thinking of hiring some former Nightstalker pilots?"

"Maybe. I haven't decided yet. If you don't want to gift me those little birds, I'll buy them off you."

"I'll get them transferred."

"Perfect, thanks."

"What are we going to do until dinner?"

"Let's go fishing."

"Sweet."

THE END

Dear Reader, thank you for purchasing Arabian Fury. If you enjoyed the book, please consider leaving a review on amazon.com

Other books by James Lawrence

 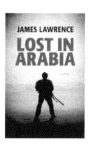